WHERE ARE MY FRIENDS AND FAMILY?

MICHAEL MORGAN

Copyright © 2024 Michael Morgan
All rights reserved
First Edition

Fulton Books
Meadville, PA

Published by Fulton Books 2024

ISBN 979-8-89221-715-6 (paperback)
ISBN 979-8-89221-716-3 (digital)

Printed in the United States of America

In loving memory of my big brother. His encouragement and help gave me the confidence to write this story. He passed away on December 5, 2023. Love you, bro.

INTRODUCTION

What would happen if you woke one day and you were an enemy of the United States? Your state had become a Confederate state. A rebel state that had seceded from the United States. A large Union Army has invaded your state of North Carolina and is marching right toward your farm. Do you fight for the life you've always known?

What would you do?

My great-great-grandfather had some decisions to make. How do I protect my family, and what will this huge army of the Union do to us? His main concern was his seventeen-year-old son, Patrick Henry. What will happen to him?

He sent his son to the Virginia Military School for an education and to be safe from the coming war. He could not have imagined his son partaking in a major battle at New Market. This was the first and only time students had been called to battle. This is a biographical story about my great-grandfather, Patrick Henry Morgan, as told by Patrick himself. The characters are mostly real, and the events are based on facts. Patrick begins his life story at seventeen years old.

Prologue

My great-grandfather, Patrick H. Morgan, was a very successful man in northeast North Carolina. He was a farmer, lawyer, sportsman, member of the North Carolina Senate, and superintendent of the United States Life-Saving Service from Cape Henry to the South Carolina line (the forerunner of the US Coast Guard). He started the first post office in Shawboro and was its first postmaster general. My great-grandfather did all of this from 1844 to 1919. He is buried in the Morgan graveyard beside his home in Shawboro, North Carolina, which still stands today.

All those accomplishments are something to be very proud of, and I certainly am proud to have a person like him in my family tree. But I believe being a cadet at VMI during the years 1862 to 1864 was his greatest achievement. To be a seventeen-year-old when the world as he knew it changed, and life-changing decisions had to be made. This was my great-grandfather's situation. It was the beginning of the most costly war the United States ever had in terms of loss of life and destruction of property. The civil war was about to begin, and brother would fight brother, friend would fight friend, and worst of all, family would fight family. The war was in your town, even in your backyard. The lands were barren as the mighty armies marched through and took what they needed to continue to fight. Looting prevailed, and nobody was safe or left untouched by this war.

I want the reader to feel the true fear of living in this time when nothing was as it was. Everything about your life was about trying to survive.

What did the common Southern man think about the reason for war?

Some people in the South were never bothered by the US government. They lived, as compared to today, very much free of the federal government.

The simple truth of the war was that the Northern states were growing rapidly in population, mostly due to immigration. The cities to the North needed money to build and enlarge so it could accommodate the influx of people. To do this, a country-wide tax was needed. The South did not have a problem with immigration as its cities were small, and the people lived mostly in rural areas. This idea of taxes paid by all was not liked by the South or necessary as far as they were concerned. The country was split up into two distinct lands. The North had control of the government in Washington, and they were making the decisions. The population of the North was expanding rapidly, and taxes were coming regardless of what the South said. The Southern states using slaves was thought by the Northern states to be economically unfair. Another concern was that the United States was growing westward, and new states were coming into the Union. The North wanted these new states to be slave-free states, and the South wanted the new states to allow slavery. So the North favored high tariffs for internal federal spending. The South did not want tariffs and opposed federal spending on internal improvements.

This is somewhat similar to the Revolutionary War with respect to the young United States, who did not like Great Britain's decision to tax them without equal representation. Massive immigration strengthened the Northern economy. The immigrant population gave the North a large source of workers who were willing to work at a lower wage. The Southern states had very few immigrants, and the population was not growing nearly as much as the Northern states, so the labor force was relatively small, and slavery played an important role in the South's workforce. There was no solution to this problem. War was enviable, as neither side would back down. The South and the North were like two separate countries, and nothing could bring them back together except one side forcing the other side back into the fold. No one thought this war would last a year, let alone almost five years, but it did and almost destroyed the United States.

WHERE ARE MY FRIENDS AND FAMILY?

Men, like my great-grandfather, were there to help build back the country. I want to honor him by telling his story based on known facts with some assumptions I added that could have happened based on letters he wrote to his father and those letters his father wrote to his son while at VMI.

All the characters' names in this book are based on real people, and the events are based on actual events. I decided to begin my great-grandfather's story in the year 1861. He was seventeen years old, and the Civil War was beginning. He was still living at home on his father's farm with his dad (Joseph B. Morgan), his mother (Ann L. Morgan), and his two brothers, Joseph W (one year old) and Francis Marion (fifteen years old), and three sisters, Elizabeth(Lizzie) Lamb (twelve years old), Ida Norman (six years old), and Lydia (nine years old). The farm was a working farm with a reported seventeen slaves registered to Joseph Morgan in 1860. Joseph was a prosperous landowner in the Currituck County of North Carolina and was well respected by the people who knew him. He often helped many neighbors out when they needed a loan or just some advice on life. Joseph's life was upended in 1861: his state, North Carolina, had now seceded from the United States. He is now a Confederate. The Union troops were now the enemy troops, and they were invaders of his land. In August of 1861, Maj. General Benjamin Butler captured Hatteras Island, and the war was closing in on Joseph and his family.

That same month, Elizabeth (Lissie) Lamb, at age twelve, passed away from diphtheria. Joseph has suffered through his children's deaths as he has lost five of his eleven children. Patrick H. Morgan was born the same day that Joseph's oldest son died, July 31, 1844. Joseph had faced death before, but in this strange new world, he knew he would face burdens and much death. This was a scary and unpredictable period to live in and raise a family. He worried most about his son Patrick. The youthful excitement of defending their new country was growing, and young men were signing up to join the Yankees or the Confederate Army. The only thing he thought he could do to protect his young son was to send him away to Virginia Military School in Lexington, Virginia, before he was taken in by the army of the North or the army of the South. But he had to pull some strings to get him in.

His Story Begins

John (John Willington, my cousin), Henry (Henry Shaw, my friend and neighbor), and I were in the swamp, fishing for white perch and catching some whoppers, when Henry asked, "What do you think of the Yankees coming our way?"

"Well," I thought for a moment and continued, "I don't know how we are going to stop them."

"We will shoot any Yankee that comes up here. We are at war," John said with passion.

"You know, guys," Henry said, "I don't think I want to kill anybody."

"Well, you might have to, as they are coming and coming with guns. Which side are you two on?" asked John.

"I'm on your side, John. I'm your cousin," I said.

"You got a bite! Reel him in, John, and let's get the rest of these fish fileted and a fire going so we can have a nice fish fry. I'm hungry."

I did not realize the time and for sure missed dinner at Aunt Nellie's house. I knew Aunt Nellie would not be happy.

"Boy, I got some good fried chicken waiting on the table there for you, and I hope you are hungry."

"I'm sorry, Aunt Nellie, but I already had fried fish with John and Henry. We caught some big ones in the swamp and fried them up good."

This wasn't the first time I did not let her know I was eating out, and she was not happy. Aunt Nellie was a house slave, and she practically raised me. I loved her as such and was very sorry.

Aunt Nellie said, "Were you out with those two hooligans last night? Those boys are in trouble. Why, last night after my church meeting, about three or four men on horses dressed in white sheets came riding up and scared everyone to death."

"You've never heard so much screaming and praying at the same time."

"I know it was those boys. I could tell by their laughing and lousy horsemanship as they nearly fell off their horses as they laughed and carried on. But I could not figure out who the other boy was. Patrick, where were you last night?"

"Aw, Aunt Nellie, I would never do something like that. Besides, I was over at my girlfriend's house. You know Mary DeFord, the prettiest girl in the county. I was having dinner with her and her family."

Aunt Nellie thought for a few seconds and then said, "Maybe that other boy was Pat Grandy, another friend you can go visit in jail in the future. Maybe it was him. You tell your pals I've got my eye on them. I just hope the congregation returns to night services, as those boys scared half of them to an early grave. Lord, have mercy. Child, you need to run with a better crowd."

"I'm sorry about that, Aunt Nellie, but I'm tired, and I have chores to get to in the morning. Good night. I was still worn out from last night's ride to the Negroes church."

The early morning part of the day was the best. The sky was clear. Everybody was out in the fields and doing their chores. I always enjoyed doing my chores around the farm. I never did any farming as we had slaves who knew how to grow good crops. I enjoyed the animals, like chickens, cows, sheep, and even the hogs, if you stood downwind of them. What a beautiful land. My best friend was Fred. He had been a slave since birth, and he was only a year younger than me, I think, as he had no birth papers. He and I were in charge of the animals with our own crew of slaves to boss around. Fred was such a good slave that Pa said that when I went off someday, he would put Fred in charge of the animals on the farm. This made Fred very proud and highly respected by the other slaves. My father always treated his slaves like ordinary workers for hire. They were paid in the form of food, housing, and medical care. Fred once told me that all the Negroes he knows wished they worked for Master Morgan.

WHERE ARE MY FRIENDS AND FAMILY?

Some days, Fred and I would lay on our backs, enjoying the clouds flowing through the sky. One day, I asked him what he would wish for if he could have anything he wanted.

He said, "I don't know, Master Pat. What would you wish for?"

I smiled and said, "I would want to travel and see the world, and maybe you could come with me, Fred. What do you think about that?"

Fred would just laugh and say, "Sounds good, Master Pat."

I would often ask my dad why we had slaves. Why did we not just hire them as workers and pay them like any other employee? This seemed to stress him as if he also struggled with slavery. My dad pointed out the problems that a freed slave would have. Most could not read or write. Most would not be hired because of their skin color, and they could not survive as free men. My pa went on to say the Negroes entered our country as slave labor and, in the Southern lands, had become an important part of the economy. I couldn't see a change being made as it would be catastrophic for the South's economy. I do believe that change should and could happen by educating slaves, but I don't see that happening in the near future.

I rode over to see my friend William (Willie) Shaw (Henry's brother). He graduated from Indian Ridge Academy (September 1, 1861) and was made a drillmaster by the governor of North Carolina. He reported to his father, Col. Henry M. Shaw, whose troops he drilled until the elder Shaw made his son decline a commission as a lieutenant in one of the companies. His pa wanted him to go to Virginia Military Institute. Colonel Shaw had already seen action at the battle of Roanoke Island. Before the war, he served in Congress from 1853–1859. He signed the Paper of Succession and was commissioned a colonel. During the battle of Roanoke Island, Colonel Shaw's troops had to retreat, and he was captured by the Yankee forces (February 10, 1862). He was later released (August 1862) at Elizabeth City. He was an important man, but not allowing Willie to accept a commission as a lieutenant did not sit well with Willie as he much preferred to fight in the war. I knew that Willie was angry about going to VMI, but I had some news for him. I went over to see Willie when he got home.

"Hi, Mrs. Shaw. Is Willie around?"

"Yes, Patrick, I'll get him. He just got home this morning. Pat, how are you doing? It's great to see you."

"Thank you, Mrs. Shaw. I am doing just fine."

Mrs. Shaw called out to Willie to come downstairs. "You have a visitor."

I hardly recognized him as he came down the stairs two at a time. He looked terribly fit and older than I remembered. "Hey, Willie." I smiled and continued, "You look like hell. I thought you wanted to join up with General Lee and fight."

"I do and will eventually. I hope, but my pa said not now. I need more military experience. I think he just wants me safe as long as possible from this war, but it might be over before I get a chance to fight."

"Well, Willie, I told your pa I will watch over you."

"What do you mean by that?" Willie thought to himself, *I don't need anybody watching over me!*

"I am going with you to VMI." I smiled really big.

"Son of a bitch, Pat, that will be great! We will soon run that school. I can show drilling and rifling."

"Hold on, Willie, we still have a few months before we go. Let's enjoy ourselves while we can because I think this war will change everything. Let's make some plans."

My dad was still mourning the death of my sister Lettie. She was only twelve years old and died from diphtheria. We were heartbroken over her death as she seemed to be getting better, and then she died. Diphtheria was going around the county badly this year, and Ma was helping to care for many of the local folks. She and Pa seemed to always have a sore throat, and Pa had night sweats and chills most nights, but they went about their business anyway. Thank God the rest of the family was healthy. One of the happiest and saddest days for my folks was the day I was born and the day my oldest brother died. Those two events occurred on the same day, July 31, 1844. My brother was three years old.

Fred and I would sneak off on our ponies and gallop to a cool creek just inside the swamp. The water was clear and felt great. You had to be careful before you jumped in because there could be an alligator lingering in there. You had to watch out for water snakes too; some can kill you, like the cottonmouth (water moccasin), but that didn't stop us from jumping in. Sometimes, it was so hot that the risk was worth it. After our swim, we would talk about what we would like to do in our life. I wanted to travel the world and see the big cities, but Fred would always just smile and say, "I hope one day you can do all that traveling, Master Pat."

I finally asked him sincerely, "What do you want, Fred? I really want to know."

He looked at me with amazement. "Master Pat, do you really want to know what I wish for?"

"Yes, I do, Fred."

His face changed into a wishful look, and he proceeded to tell me all. "Well, Master Pat, all I wish for was a nice piece of land that I could call my own and that I could go anywhere in the county freely without needing permission."

You see, Fred was a young slave. He was a young slave owned by my pa. I think he was about the same age as me, but he had no birth certificate, so nobody knew how old he was. It seemed to me that Fred had it made. He had a good job, food, medical care, and a place to live on a beautiful farm. But I realized he did not have a great life because he was bound to this farm and to me. I could sell him like a piece of property. I understood this, but I let it go and just enjoyed another swim.

My pa was not happy about the Yankees coming our way, and he told me that I was not old enough to fight. He did not know that Willie and I were planning to join up with the Confederate Army. We had decided that when the Confederate Army came to our town, we would sneak out and join up. We even had our goodbye notes to our parents written.

Pa believed in the fight to secure our way of life and that no one had the right to tell us what to do. We have never asked the government for help, and they have never offered any help. That is the way he would like to keep it. Pa had no contact with the federal government other than postal service and voting.

Pa told me he was sending me to Virginia Military Institute this summer (1862). Apparently, the colonel (Henry M. Shaw) has some pull, as I guess that is how I got into VMI, even though my pa was a very important man in the county. I'm sure that was in my favor also. I went over to Willie's to see what he was up to. His ma told me he was out in the outhouse, so I said, "I'll just go over and wait for him."

I knocked on the door and asked him how long he expected to be in there. He started whining about how we couldn't go to war together and kill the Yankees. I was actually relieved a little, as the idea of killing was not pleasant to me. Finally, I told Willie to shut up and stop whining as I reminded him I was going with him to VMI.

He jumped out of the outhouse, yelling, "That's right! We can learn how to fight and then really kick some Yankee butt."

I said, "You're damn right we can. Now please pull your pants up before your sisters see you." My concern for Willie was whether he could stay in the school long enough to graduate, as his attitude toward school was not good. He always said school was just a way to avoid work on the farm. I liked school because I got to see Mary (my girlfriend) often. I thought I would marry her someday in my dreams. But schoolwork was not too hard, as I especially liked math.

As the days passed, the Yankees seemed to be coming up the coast toward us, and the Confederate forces couldn't stop them. The word here is that General Lee was too spread out to send reinforcements to take back and hold the coastal region of North Carolina. The Yankees were determined to take the waterways and close them off to prevent the Southern blockade runners from getting supplies to the Confederate Army.

My pa got the family together, which included Uncle James (brother to Pa), Uncle George, who was Ma's brother, and all the children. He sat us down and described the situation as it is now.

Pa started talking, "According to the latest news, the Yankees have captured Hatteras Island and hold it now. The Yankees will be marching north toward us. I want all of you to be aware of the possible appearance of Yankee patrols, so stay on your farms and don't venture out alone. If you see any Yankees, stay away from them."

WHERE ARE MY FRIENDS AND FAMILY?

Uncle George (Ma's brother) joined the Confederate Army and was reporting to them in October. This did not make Ma happy as she told him he was too old to fight, but Uncle George was determined to fight for what he believed in. The war seemed very real to me now. Uncle George took my father aside and asked him if he would care for his family if something should happen to him, and, of course, my pa said he would. My ma cried the rest of the day.

As the days went by, all of my friends were trying to figure out what to do. Pat Grandy went to join the Confederate Army at Richmond. Henry Bradshaw, the younger brother to William, studied medicine under Dr. Williams. Pat Woods was coming to VMI with us. Dorsey Sanderland joined the Confederate Army. Those who stayed behind had to swear allegiance to the Yankees. Some of the boys went to the Yankee Army in order to get the bounty they offered for joining.

In February 1862, the Yankees had taken Roanoke Island. By March, the Yankees marched into Beaufort at night, and the residents woke up under Yankee control. The Battle of New Bern caused more than a thousand casualties. New Bern became the capital of the Union of North Carolina.

My friends were actually fighting over which side to take. I had many fights with my friends over me going to VMI and not joining in the war. Some of my friends went to the Yankees, and others to the Confederates. Currituck County soon became a zone of occupation by the Yankees. Every able-bodied White man had only three choices to make, and all three were bad. Take a loyalty pledge to the Yankees that you will abide by their rules and make the best of the situation, or you could sneak across the lines and join, or be conscripted into the Confederate Army, or go and collect a bounty by enlisting in the Union volunteer regiments. Those who joined the Yankee volunteer regiments patrolled the local areas, looking for Southern guerillas who often were people they knew. The local folks in these volunteer units were called buffaloes and were, more often than not, bushwhackers and thugs who terrorized the local folk like my pa by stealing and settling old scores.

I was glad to be leaving and starting my education at VMI. Pa was worried that I might be stopped by the Yankees, but each checkpoint okayed my travel papers, and I arrived at school with no problems. The school was alive with cadets drilling, and the grounds were immaculately clean and neat. My first order of business was to report to the administration building to pay my tuition and the other items I would need for my schooling. These were a few of the items I paid for:

Tuition	$60
Room furniture	$2.50
Washing (cleaning cost of uniforms and such)	$12.83
Doctor's fee	$5
Music	$5
Board	$107
White pants	$12
White jacket	$8

It totaled up to $348.29 for the half year of school.

The next place I went was to report to the headmaster or commandant. He assigned me my room (no. 45).

When I arrived at my room, I was greeted by four upperclassmen. They welcomed me very warmly and told me to write down on a sheet of paper my name, county, state I was from, Virginia Military School, and my class year. They then grabbed me and tied my hands together and made me put my hands over my knees. Can it get any worse? Yes, it can. One of them slid a stick between my arms and legs. Then all four lifted me up and rotated me till my face was on the floor and began to whip me with a bayonet scabbard. They whipped me once for every letter and number I had written. They nearly twisted my arms off. This treatment is called "bucking."

They told me, "You better not whine about it, or you will be labeled a wimp for the rest of your time at school." They all shook my hand and said, "Welcome. You will be a great cadet and make VMI proud." Then they left. I cried like a baby, and as soon as my arms got some feeling back, I was leaving.

Thank the Lord, a guy came in a few hours later, and it was my future roommate, Sam Atwill.

"It looks like you just got bucked," Sam said with a little grin. "It's okay. You can cry all you want. I won't rat on you."

I cried pretty hard myself.

"It hurt like hell, didn't it?" Sam said with some sympathy. "We all go through it."

"It is good to see you, Sam," I said, with a tear in the corner of my eye. "I miss home terribly."

"Me too," Sam said.

"William(Willie) Shaw is coming to school and should be around here somewhere. He should have gotten here a day or two before me. It will be good to have Willie with us," I said. "He will be a good soldier and roommate." I explained to Sam that Willie had been in camp with his pa (Col. Henry M. Shaw), drilled his new recruits, and had great experience in army life. "He will do well here with his knowledge and confidence."

"Hey, Sammy, how have you been? I've missed you."

"Well, if it isn't Robert Brockenbrough, mister cadet himself."

"You know, Sammy, I can drill all day with the best of them."

"Hey, Robert, I want you to meet our new roommate. This here is Patrick H. Morgan. He's from Shawboro, North Carolina, where all the Yankees are, and he was just about to tell some stories of what is going on down in Currituck County. Go on, Pat."

"Well, the enemy makes raids on my pa's farm. They take the animals and crops needed to feed the Yankee troops without consideration for the people who live there. Just before I left home, they burned some buildings on the farm and stole horses, carts, Negroes, salt, and about anything they wanted."

"Well, Pat, just wait until we get in this war, yea," said Robert. "We will kill every one of those Northern bastards."

"Quiet, Robert. You want Old Spex to hear you and get your first demerit? You know cussing is not allowed."

"Who is Old Spex?"

"I'll tell you, Pat, he is the top guy around here as far as schooling is concerned. He looks like an old owl with those glasses, and he hears everything, so look out for him. Looky here. Here comes another roommate."

Sam Atwill wanted to give him a proper introduction. "Pat, here is Henry Thomas Wood."

Henry smiled and said, "Come on, Sam, I've known Pat for years. How're you doing, Pat? Great to see you and have you as a roommate."

"Well," Sam continued, "Henry, I didn't know you had any friends outside of the academy. You know, Pat, we are forced to tolerate him."

"Don't start with me on the first day, Sam." Henry frowned. "Those damn Yankees gave me a hard time. They called me a little schoolboy and said, 'Hurry along to school.'" Henry was pissed.

"Don't worry, Henry," said Sam, "we will get a shot at killing some Yanks."

"I hope so, as I am leaving if we don't. Say, Pat, did you get bucked?"

That brought a laugh from the group.

"I sure did. How about you?"

"Yea, they beat the shit out of me with the number of letters in my name."

"Careful, Henry, cussing is not permitted on campus. You don't want to get a demerit."

I asked, "Why do they keep count?"

"They sure do. If you get ten demerits or less, you get a fifteen-day furlong in the summer. Believe me, that furlong is a very precious item."

"Hey, guys, let's get out of this room and see the campus and maybe go into town because I am thinking tomorrow school begins, and life as we know it may be over."

"What do you mean our life will be over?" I thought to myself, *What have I gotten myself into?*

Sam just laughed and said, "Come on, guys. Let's go."

WHERE ARE MY FRIENDS AND FAMILY?

Lexington was a nice city full of people. I have not seen so many people in one place. Some of them didn't look too friendly, so I asked Sam, "Am I right to think some of these people don't like us?"

"You are correct, my friend. Some of these people don't believe the state of Virginia should have seceded. Fools if you ask me. It's good to stay in groups when you visit town."

As soon as we reached the city, we heard a commotion out in the street. Three guys circled around a person who looked vaguely familiar. He had a cadet uniform on, so it did not matter who it was. We came running over to help him. By the time we got there, two of the men were on the ground. The third guy took off when he saw us coming. Sam got there first and asked the cadet if he was all right.

The cadet looked at him and said, "I'm fine. Do you want some of this ass-kicking too?"

When I got over to Sam, I could see the cadet plainly. I just laughed and said, "Boys, meet our fifth roommate. Let me introduce you all to Cadet William Shaw. My best mate from my hometown."

"Okay, Pat, let's not hug and kiss now. Who are these boys? Oh, I know Henry Woods," Willie said with a big smile, "but who are the rest of these clowns?"

"Cadet Sam Atwill, a pleasure to meet you, William."

"Cadet Robert Brockenbrough at your service, Cadet William."

"You boys can call me Willie. I'm glad to meet you, guys, and thanks for your help even though I was doing pretty well without it."

"Come on, Willie, you can hang out with us and protect us from these Northern sympathizers. Let's go get a drink," I suggested.

"Sounds good to me," said Willie. "I've never turned one down yet. I knew that our room would be the best in the barracks as we all hit it off well."

The first day at VMI was tough. This was the schedule at the college:

Up at 5:00 a.m., three minutes to dress
Drill at 5:30–7:00 a.m.
Breakfast at 7:00 a.m.
Squad drills at 9:00–10:00 a.m.

Study hall or recitation(classes) till 12:00 p.m.
Lunch at 12:00–1:00 p.m.
Study or recitation at 1:00–4:00 p.m.
Squad drills at 5:00–6:00 p.m.
Come back and go to the dress parade at 6:15 p.m.
Dinner at 7:00–8:00 p.m.
Lights out at 10:00 p.m.

It was very strict, and you cannot be late, or you get a demerit.

I had no free time to even write to my parents. The courses were tough. We had French, Latin, geography, composition, and declamation.

My favorite subject was mathematics. I seemed to get angles and numbers easily. I knew that my math instructor had suggested to the class that in artillery, mathematics was very important. That feels like an exciting place for me to be. As he said, a good artillery unit could save a lot of soldiers in a battle.

Another horrific duty we had to do was guard duty. You must do four guard duties during the day and four guard duties at night every month. Each duty was eight and a half hours of walking. Here I am, with nowhere to go in the middle of a civil war, walking miles with a gun that weighs ten pounds and is not even loaded. What a pain. Everything and every drill was for the purpose of making us better soldiers.

Sam was telling us the story of a new cadet named James Reid. He had just gotten to school and was resting in his room after dinner. His roommates had all gone to town. The corporal of the guard came for him to go on guard duty at an outer post and was very particular in telling him to let no one pass without the countersign, but the corporal gave him no load to put in his gun. While he was on guard duty, about twenty-five cadets came down and wanted to take his gun, but he stuck one of them with his bayonet (but not very hard as he knew it was a trick to frighten him) and drove them off. They came back later with guns that were loaded and took his gun. The corporal came back and made a big fuss, saying he would be responsible for the neglect of duty. James was not taking this assault well and explained to the corporal how twenty-five men with guns could easily take one man's gun. The corporal said, "You must be court-martialed," and sent him to the guard house, but in fact, it was Profs. Wise and Semmes's room. Kept him for most of the night and day but realized he was not fooled by their prank and let him out. Our roommates are important for protection from the older cadets, and we, rats, need to stay in a pack to protect ourselves. But the older cadets must have decided they needed to get back at James for not falling for their bad prank. On Wednesdays and Saturdays, our clothes come in from the laundry. Well, last Wednesday night, the clothes all came in, and an old cadet by the name of Exall ordered James to carry his box of clothes up the stairs to his room. James had had enough of this harassment from the older cadets, so he pitched in and thrashed him pretty badly. All the other rats (first-year cadets) thought James was a hero. Unfortunately, that was not the end of hostilities. Exall got some friends of the same feather and caught him, at least jumped upon him suddenly Monday night as he was coming off guard duty and his gun lying carelessly across his shoulder. They tied him up and hung him over the door until he passed out. Yesterday, I met James on the quad, and he looked like he had been in a fight. His eye was black and blue, and his pinky finger was bent sideways. I asked him what happened.

He said, "I met two of the old cadets that jumped me the other night. They said they wanted to fight, but they said they would see fair play, so I beat one up at a time all to pieces, knocked one's teeth down his throat, and at least two of them. I only got this eye shiner and a crooked pinky. I hope they leave me alone now." James mumbled, "If I had known in Lynchburg how I was to be treated, I never would have consented to come. But since I have passed through it, I don't think I will be molested anymore."

A few days later, General Smith allowed the same fellows who mistreated James to resign for nearly killing a rat named Cocke, a son of Philip St. George Cocke. All had gone home some days ago. I believe the older cadets had a new respect for old James, but they still treated us pretty badly. Ten cadets deserted the other day, and ten or twelve were planning to leave soon. There was a rumor going around that all cadets eighteen and older would be taken as transcripts. I don't know how true it was. If true, the institute would be broken up unless they were exempted by Congress.

When I first entered the institute, I liked it very well, but in the last two or three weeks, I had become very dissatisfied. Among other things, I did not get enough to eat. My seat was in the middle of a long table. At breakfast, a pitcher of milk was put at both ends of the table, and by the time it got to me, it was empty, so I had to eat dry bread the same at supper. Today, I was so hungry that I ate a piece of rotten beef, although it smelled very bad, and a piece of bread. Since then, I had thrown up several times and still felt very badly in my stomach. My only resource was to buy some apples and fill up with them. Colonel Whitwell, who was in charge of the commissary, said the fare would be better in a week or so. The past few weeks had been difficult, and I had not been able to go to class or study well. My grades were failing, and I was never feeling well for the last couple of weeks in drills. We had been double-quicked until I could go no further. The demerits continued to come my way as I could not continue to drill day and night. I was seeing Dr. Madison for treatment, but it was not improving much. Dr. Madison said this morning that the fare here was calculated to give anybody typhoid fever.

Gen Smith, I believe, would omit some of the demerits as I wrote up my reasons for missing class and drills. I was able to obtain the doctor's orders to rest for a few days, and I believe that the general would have sympathy for me and reduce the demerits. I believe Major Shipp (who had gone off to be married and would be back in a week) would excuse the rest of my demerits (I hope).

The doctor's orders for me to rest were a godsend. I was feeling much better and was catching up on my classwork. I learned so rapidly lately that they had put me in company drill, which I was very glad of, for it was nothing as hard as squad drill.

I was made orderly in my room. An orderly was a cadet who was detailed every Sunday morning. He swept out the room, brought water, and was responsible for noises. One night, some of the boys in my room (Henry and Robert) made noises after taps. I, as the orderly, was reported as making noise after taps (after taps were after the lights had been put out). All of them denied making any noise, so I, as the orderly, took the blame and the five demerits. I had a talk with my buddy Willie, and he assured me this would not happen again. Willie had a way of controlling our room. I didn't think I would be getting any more demerits in the future.

I was getting very tired of VMI. I wrote Pa a letter telling him this, and I would a great deal rather be with him on the farm than here, especially as he had no one to assist him. I knew he had a great deal to do. If the army marched out, I could meet him (Pa) at a certain place, and we could go home together. Just a thought. Love, your son, Cadet PH Morgan.

I hadn't been at the institute very long when a great deal of excitement began to build as news came that the Yankees were about to enter the city of Staunton. Academic duties were suspended, and our time was devoted to three drills a day, preparing ourselves to meet the invader should he attempt to drive us away from VMI. General Smith told us he intended to lead us out to meet them if they came a thousand strong. He had provisions cooked for us to take with us on our way to Lynchburg or Richmond if they came too large a force for us to meet them. I assure you, I was very sorry when I heard they weren't coming to Staunton. General Smith wrote to General Jackson, tendering him our services. General Jackson replied that he would keep us as a reserve body and that we could be of immense service to him. He would call upon us when he wanted us, and we must keep ourselves constantly in readiness. I must say, in the midst of the excitement, I was hoping he would call on us to help defend our homes against the invader. The Yankees were going to Charlottesville now, and all our cannons were sent there. I was sorry to see our cannons sent off to fight without us. I had practiced on those cannons and had grown quite fond of them. These four cannons were made especially for the VMI cadets. They were donated to VMI by President Zachary Taylor in 1850. These four guns were christened as "the four apostles: Matthew, Mark, Luke, and John." They were given these names by Col. William Pendleton and the seminary students because "they spoke a powerful language." Again, academics were suspended, and the professors did not expect us to have classwork as all our time was taken up with drilling and preparing for a Yankee advance toward Staunton. The cadets might be called up to march to Stauntan in support of General Jackson. Much to our liking, six stagecoaches loaded with young college ladies were coming from Staunton this Sunday evening because their college was evacuated to Lexington. We (cadets) got orders to march out to Staunton early Monday morning. Can you believe our rotten luck? Our town was filled with beautiful ladies from Staunton, and we were going to Staunton maybe to fight. I was not happy about this twist of fate, but almost everybody else was happy to march away from hordes of beautiful college ladies in order to get a shot off at a Yankee. No shots were ever fired by a VMI cadet during this march.

We returned to the VMI yesterday after one of the most toilsome marches ever endured by an army. Let me tell you, after we left Staunton, our hardships began. We marched every day without even a day's rest for ten or twelve days, always averaging eighteen miles and often twenty to twenty-five. One day, the day of the battle at McDowell, we marched forty miles, marching from early morning until two or three in the evening. We drove the enemy before us all the time. General Jackson's men were in the rear of the army, so we did not get in the fight. The battle was fought by General Johnson's army. The corps of cadets were nearly all broken down. We were lame with sore feet. I could scarcely walk at times. My feet hurt so much. A number of us threw our shoes away and walked barefoot over some of the loftiest mountains in western Virginia. For days, we saw nothing but mountains, and often it rained hard as we couldn't even see the mountains. Some nights, I would lie down, and in the morning, I would get up with my clothes soaked and a chill that took most of the morning sun to cure. The volunteers, who were a group of young boys (fifteen to nineteen) and older men (some as old as fifty years), all said that the march through Western Virginia was the hardest they had endured since the war. When we returned to Staunton, we were dismissed. General Jackson went on down the valley. We all hoped he would drive those Yanks across the Potomac. That was my first march, and welcome to the cadet's life, I guess.

We were always ready if needed by our country. That was expected. The constant classwork was not. Life as a cadet was not going to be easy.

During my first six months of school, my class was referred to as rats. At times, the upperclassmen would come into a rat room in the middle of the night and clean out the rats. Throw us out of the room along with our books, clothes, and sometimes a bed. This went on for the first six months, and hopefully, things would calm down eventually. I really hated those upperclassmen until one day, a group of us (rats) went down into town. We stopped into a shop for a soda, and as we were enjoying our sodas, a group of older men started calling us names like baby troopers and dirty rebel babies. The worst remark was "Your pa's sent you here to stay out of the war. Cowards you are."

We were not going to take that, so we threw some name-calling back at them. They did not take it as well as we took their insults and came at us. We stood our ground, and the yelling and name-calling continued until we drew a crowd with half the people on our side and half on the Northern sympathizer bastards' side. When this big party started, Henry Woods took off to the college to get help. He came back with 150 cadets with loaded muskets ready to fight. The party was over, and I knew then that everyone in the cadet corps had each other's back.

This was not the first time this happened. An old cadet told us the story. In early April 1861, unrest among the people of the community provoked an incident. On Saturday afternoon, attempts were made to raise two flags in Lexington, one for recession and one for staying with the Union, and among citizens assembled on the streets, there was a strong feeling. Since it was a free afternoon for the cadets, many were in town and were thrown into contact with persons whose sentiments differed greatly from those of a VMI cadet. The excitement increased when an extremist drew a revolver and knife on a squad of cadets, and though the difficulty was quelled by onlookers who intervened, word spread quickly to barracks that a group of cadets was in danger. From the barracks, the already aroused cadets, with rifles in hand, began to run toward the town but were instantly headed off by

Old Spex (VMI superintendent), who ordered them to return to the barracks. The corps was assembled, and the superintendent (General Smith), still very upset with the cadet corps for charging to the city, urged old Hickory (Maj. Thomas Jonathon Jackson, you rats might know him better as General Thomas Stonewall Jackson) to speak to the corps. The old cadet (as we called Major Jackson) thought for a moment. We didn't know what he was going to say because, based on his teaching style, he was not much of an orator. Major Jackson stood there, looking over us apparently, trying to think of what to say. Finally, I believe he said, "Military men make short speeches, and for myself, I am no hand at speaking anyhow. The time for war has not yet come, but it will come that soon, and when it does come, my advice is to draw the sword and throw away the scabbard." What a story. I didn't know General Jackson taught here.

The old cadet said, "Oh yea, he taught here for years up to 1861 when he was called to duty. He served as an instructor in artillery tactics and military training for all cadets. He was a terrible teacher, but he knew how to fight a battle."

Boy, was Old Spex (General Smith) upset at the corps for going to town with loaded guns. He declared that the town of Lexington was off-limits for cadets indefinitely, which was a good thing since a portion of the population was Northern sympathizers and did not like our military school being near their town. What a sight to see 150 cadets with loaded muskets ready for battle running into town. No question, the cadets were restless and ready for a fight.

The schedule of drills and classwork gave me no time to even write home. The exams were upon us, and study time was difficult to find. I was so nervous I couldn't even spit on exam day. When I entered the exam room, there were about twenty subs and professors sitting in a row. In the center sat Old Spex, as big as life, resembling an old owl with a standing collar and a pair of specs on, but I would not say anything about the looks of this venerable gentleman, for he certainly is as good-looking as any monkey you ever saw with a mouth sharp enough to pick peas out of a porter bottle. But enough of this, for you know, I was badly scared being in his presence while he was testing me. The examinations were tough, but I think I did pretty well as I suspected I surprised Old Spex with my answers. At least, I hope I did. Who cares? They were over now, and we had a holiday until next week. I was so happy, and what a relief. I heard the drum beating, which meant it was time for a dress parade. I would be floating off my feet as I marched today, knowing exams were over and we got four glorious days off. The sad part was I couldn't afford to go home. Even if I had the money to get home, the word was out that you wouldn't get through the Yankee lines. Communications to the eastern Carolinas have been controlled by the Yankees, and Willie, Henry, and I could not write to our folks, which was not good since we often needed money. I mean, also to know that the family was doing well.

I received a letter from my cousin, which I read to my roommates. The actual letter was dated July 2, 1862.

> Forestville, N.C.
> Friend Pat,
>
> I was in Currituck a few days ago and saw your father. He gave me a letter to bring out for you which I have this day mailed to you. He requested me to write to you and tell you where to write to him at so that he could get it. If you write to him and enclose it to me at Murfreesboro NC. I will endeavor to get it to him. Say to col. Shaw and Mr. Woods' sons that if they will do the same I will try to forward their letters on for them. I heard that Pat Grandy was killed in Richmond. Poor fellow I am sorry for him, he was a brave little fellow. Write soon as I shall be in Murfreesboro in about six days.
>
> Yours very respectfully,
> D.W. (Cousin)

All of us were very sad to hear about Pat Grandy. He was so well-liked by everyone, but he was determined to defend his country from the invaders. I used to tell him, "Grandy, you need to grow taller if you want to be a soldier." Boy, that would get him mad as a wet hornet. It's true that the short ones usually have the worst temperament. He was a fine friend and will be missed.

The best news we could have gotten was we could write to our families back home. I sent a short note home telling everyone I was doing well, and even though school was very difficult, I was doing okay. "Tell everyone I love them and to write to me," I added.

Every letter took weeks to sometimes a month to get to me or to get home. The summer here was unbearably hot, and drilling every day was exhausting. The only reprieve we got was on one of the hottest days, we were at a dress parade in the afternoon sun when a cadet fell over right in the middle of drilling. He had fainted and dropped his musket (which weighed about ten pounds) on his foot. Of course, everybody stopped marching as his body was lying flat out among us. I wish it was me, but after a couple of quick thinking, cadets rushed to him and picked him up. Instead of taking him to the barracks, which was just as near as Major Williamson's house, they were very cunning and took him to the latter as old Tom (Major Williamson) has two very pretty daughters. As soon as they entered the house, the young ladies put water on the unconscious cadet's face and bathed his temples with cologne. In about two minutes, he came too and soon after came back to the barracks. He looked like a cat that swallowed the canary. Everybody wanted to know about the girls and what happened. But just as he was about to tell us, a servant came in with a waiter. In his hand, with a white cloth over it, was a note to the cadet with the compliments of Mrs. Williamson. Now you could imagine what was under that cloth besides having the compliments of two beautiful young ladies that you never knew before. That cadet smiled and would not tell us a thing about his experience with the young ladies. Well, if this is the way one gets paid for fainting at a dress parade, I will certainly try to break my foot tomorrow evening and then fall down, but before I do this, I will make a bargain with two fellows to have some chalk prepared for the

WHERE ARE MY FRIENDS AND FAMILY?

occasion and as soon as I fall to rub it on my face and hands and then take me to Major Williamson's or Colonel Gilham's. It makes no difference as both of them have pretty daughters and are equally distant from the parade ground, neither over fifteen yards. I just didn't have the balls to do something like that, but everybody was soaked with sweat after that parade march, so much so we even had to pay extra to have our dress uniforms cleaned, which was not paid for in our regular wash allotment. This was extra money some of us did not have. In our room after the drill, we were all bitching about the heat, and in came an older cadet (drill instructor), and he was looking pretty upset. He told us that the young cadet who fainted was taken to the commandant's house because the two cadets who took him there wanted to meet the commandant's daughters, who were fifteen and sixteen years old. Well-planned maneuver. These cadets were creative and smart. Just in case anyone else thinks about fainting or dropping a musket on their foot, they will not go to the commandant's house. They will go to the barracks or the infirmary. The drill instructor smiled as he walked away.

In the few months I've been here, I have met some good cadets. Moses Ezckiel wanted to be an artist and was very good at drawing. I think he had a future in art. I hoped so, as he ranked at the bottom of his class. Jack Stanard apparently held the record for the most demerits in a year (fifty-plus). John Early was the nephew of General Jubal Early and Jacob Imboden, the younger brother of General John Imboden. Robert Wise was the son of a past governor of Virginia. There were a lot of sons and brothers of important people of the confederacy. People might think these cadets were here to avoid fighting, but they would be wrong. All were eager for battle. They were stuck here as cadets. Jack Stanard had proven that even with fifty-plus demerits, you were not getting kicked out, so you could join up with General Lee and the Southern army. You had to have permission from your parents to leave the school.

I could say with no hesitation that the situation here was deteriorating. In the town of Lexington, the price of food was going up, and that meant the food for us cadets was going down in the amount we got to eat. I was in town last week, looking for some fruit, which was in short supply at the school. Peaches were twenty-five cents a dozen, apples twenty cents, and watermelons were one dollar and twenty-five cents each. It was very hard for me to buy on my two-dollar-monthly allowance. I needed to send a letter home soon to ask for a larger allowance and, of course, ask how the family was doing.

General Smith had given some cadets furloughs to go home and provide their winter clothing. The general was concerned that the cloth he needed would be delayed by the Northern blockades. Now winter was here, and it had been one of the coldest ones I had ever been through. I sent a letter to Pa asking for some extra money and some thick socks. I didn't know when he would receive the letter, but I hoped it would be sooner than later. But one thing was for sure: we would never stop drilling until, as the saying goes, "Hell freezes over," which would be okay as, at least, it would be warmer. Cadets were dropping like flies with fevers and colds from guard duty and constant drilling. It was very cold late at night and early in the morning, wearing only my white uniform. I nearly froze when I went on guard duty at night (every fourth night). Since I received the blankets from home, I have been very comfortable at night. Pa said in his letter, "As to your freezing on post at night, it seems to me the woolen clothes you carried ought to protect you." I never brought any woolen clothes with me. The only woolen thing I brought was the cloth coat that I put in the arsenal soon after I came here, and there were about seventy-five trunks on top of mine. But I went in yesterday and got Willie and Sam to help me dig it out. I found my trunk and got my coat. That coat was very warm, but I was not allowed to wear that coat on guard duty. But Henry (roommate) had bought a very good overcoat, which I could wear at night on guard duty as it kept me quite comfortable. I think I could get along as far as clothes were concerned.

I had been named section marcher to the eighth section, fourth class math. The duty of a section marcher is to call the roll of his section every time it goes to recite, to march the section in, to report all absentees, to be responsible for all trifling and talking in ranks, etc. I was getting some respect from my math instructors. I know this from the job of section marcher, which they bestowed on me. This was important as I had a good chance of getting into artillery. Speaking of fare, I could not get milk or bread. The only thing you could buy up here were apples, and you had to live on them. At breakfast this morning, I took a small piece of bread for my dinner and was reported for carrying provisions from the hall. That was pretty hard.

I received a box with clothes, skates, a cap cover, a cake, and apples from home. What a treat. I wrote back to Ma and Pa.

Dear Pa,

You need not trouble yourself about sending me anything to eat, as probably in a box of cake. I would get two or three to eat as everyone in the room wants a cake, and it is impossible to leave the cake in the room without someone eating it. We are all hungry, and I don't mind sharing. Don't worry about me as I will see a servant about getting something to eat or apply to change my seat at the dining table. I know the fare we get is not sufficient for the season. I think I will wait till Christmas to come home as I have much studying to do to make up for the sickness I had of late. I feel much better now, so I will endeavor to get caught up on my studies and see you at Christmas. I had worked myself up to the second section math, but because of my sickness, I fell so far back that I could not keep up with it, and I was transferred to the eighth section. While I was sick, the class went over a great deal that I did not understand, and I had to study very hard to understand it.

I, however, do very well in French and geography. The way geology is taught is a very good one. Colonel Williamson (professor) sends one of us up to the blackboard and tells us to draw the map of such a country or state with all of its rivers, towns, etc. It was very hard for me at first, but I can draw a pretty good map now. In French, I have gone through the grammar and will begin to read Gil Blas on Monday. I make the max or within a few tenths of it every week. You may not understand me when I say tenths. The way they mark us is this, if you make a perfect recitation, they mark you thirty-tenths or three whole ones and skin you by tenths accordingly as you recite. They love to skin the rats.

They have not commenced to heat up the barracks yet. Some say they will not commence until Christmas. It is very cold getting up at five o'clock in the morning without any fire and going out and drilling for an hour. The only good thing about cold weather is the river beside the school freezes over, and some of us go ice-skating down the river for a mile or two. It's a freeing moment to get away from the redundant routine of being a cadet.

I have made an arrangement with a servant to supply me with some chicken, some butter, and some good bread every five days in a week at one dollar and twenty-five cents. I intend to get him down to a dollar. If he furnishes me in the mess hall, they will report me for a private dish. I, therefore, stay away from dinner, and he brings it to me in my room. He has furnished me for four days, and I would owe him after today a dollar and twenty-five cents, and I only have fifty cents left. I will get him to trust me and pay him at the end of the month. I have made my money hold out right well. I brought eight dollars here with me. You sent me ten dollars, which made eighteen dollars. I paid seven dollars for a bed, seventy-five cents for a broom, a dollar for a water bucket, and a dollar to get my gun cleaned (it was so rusty that I could do nothing with it, and I was obliged to have it cleaned, or I would have been reported every time I went on the drill), a dollar loan to Sam, and fifty cents to the Soldier's Aid Society up town, which left me about four dollars and fifty cents with which I had bought apples, cakes, etc., at different times when I was very hungry.

I have made my money go as far as possible because I know you have no money to waste. I do not think I could have stood the fare much longer if it had not been for your kind offer. I began to feel weak in the legs, dizzy in the eyes, a violent headache, and a feeling of emptiness in the stomach. I had this feeling nearly all the time and still have it slightly, but I feel a great deal better since I have been buying food from the old Negro. I am still fifteen pounds under my normal weight. There is a report among the boys that General Smith is going to give us coffee and ham. If so, I will buy no more dinners. It may be only a rumor for all I know, but I think it is very probable for General Smith, certainly, to have more feeling than to feed us on bread and milk all winter.

Tell Jodie I will be bringing him a special gift. Tell Ma I can't wait for Christmas dinner, and, Pa, I am coming to help you as much as I can on the farm and talk to you about my need for a bigger allowance.

Your loving son,
Cadet Patrick H. Morgan

I received another letter from Pa. All my roommates wanted to hear the news. Excitement. The actual letter was dated January 28, 1863.

My dear son,

It has been a long time since we have had a letter from you. The last one was dated the 16th of November last. We heard from you by Albert (friend) who got safely home, but destroyed all the letters he brought with him for fear of falling into the hands of enemies. He reported you tolerably well—but gives a horrid description of your fare, and seems very glad to get home even under the circumstances.

Your Uncle James has again been driven from his home by the shelling of his premises, and together with his family is now residing with us. Albert is going to school to Mr. Lowe, who now has a very large school. Since I last wrote to you we have had distressing intelligence of the death of your uncle George. He was killed at Fredericksburg. His family is in great distress.

They are making arrangements to move back to Currituck and reside with William Dozier, who was recently married to Miss Arnett Barnard. Your Ma is in deep distress in consequence of her brother's death. She takes it very hard indeed. Otherwise we are getting along about as we have been for the last eighteen months.

The enemy occasionally makes raids upon us and plunder and destroy our property. A few weeks ago they came over to Indian Town and burned all the buildings on Dr. Marchant's place, opposite where he used to live, together with the academy, and plundered several citizens, taking horses, carts, negroes, salt and &c. They have since removed to Shiloh and have made their headquarters at Elizabeth City. One of their officers, a Captain Sanders was killed in the street the night of the 5th inst.

The diphtheria has been very prevalent this winter. I believe I wrote to you of the death of two of Mr. Baxter's children. Now I have to inform you of the death of (Suda) Shaw of the same horrible disease. It was a heart rending scene to witness the distress of the family. I deeply sympathize with the bereaved parents, but for Suda, we know she is better off. She is beyond the reach of harm, safe in her heavenly father's arms. Jodie (Patrick's younger brother) has been strongly threatened with the same disease, if indeed he has not had it in modified form. All of us have had sore throats and your Ma has been doctoring for diphtheria. All are however better now. Lili and Ida are going to school and Jodie is playing around the house as lively as ever. He has grown very much since you saw him, and talks quite plain. You would hardly know him.

I write this my dear son hoping it may reach you soon, knowing you will be glad to hear from home and hoping soon to hear from you. You cannot imagine how anxious we are to hear from you, and surely you would write much oftener than you do. What can be the matter? Is it that you do not write or does your letters miscarry? I know not the cause, but whatever it may be, should be very glad if it could be remedied. I know not how to direct you more than I have. There are so many changes. I received one letter from Mr. Lassiter from Mr. Boro. Since then I learn he has sold out and removed, so you must seek for information and opportunities and neglect no possible chance of letting us not hearing from you. I have committed you unto him that is able to keep you, and I forget not my prayers morning and night to beseech Him to care for you, to preserve and keep you from all evil and harm, and restore you again to the bosom of the family, if it can accord with His blessed will. All send their love.

Your father,
Jos. B. Morgan

I prayed for my family every day for their safety from disease and those damn Yankees. I had written Pa, I swore, but the letters were not arriving to him. Of course, Albert had to burn the letters for fear the Yankees thought he was carrying Confederate notes. I felt terrible knowing that my family might think I didn't love or miss them. I wished I could go home when I pleased, but the trip was too dangerous, and the school wanted us here as the war was coming our way. There was a time, the old cadets said, when a cadet had over fifty demerits, he was shipped out. Last year, we had thirty or more cadets dismissed for having over fifty demerits. Some of these thirty cadets got those demerits in just six months. The school could fill their spots right away with new people. Even Colonel Gilham's son was sent home. But now the Pickens are small as most men and boys are being conscripted or have joined the Confederate Army. Now you have to commit murder to be dismissed. That is why some cadets were just deserting and going home as one cadet, we all know, had over a hundred demerits, and he was still here. Cadets cannot leave the institute unless their father says he can, or they are dismissed by the institute.

Willie took the news that his younger sister had died very hard. I've never seen him weep as he did when he heard the news. He heard the news from my letter as his father's letter had not reached him yet. Everyone in our room tried to console him but to no avail.

WHERE ARE MY FRIENDS AND FAMILY?

He wanted to go home, but the school was fearful we might need to fight as the Yankees were advancing into our valley (Shenandoah Valley). This is the breadbasket of the South and critical to the war effort. The Yankees shall never take the valley. We were excited that we might get in a battle or two yet. The cadets were ready.

With the war brewing ever closer to us, there was still classroom work to be done, and exam days were coming.

As the war progressed, it started to seriously affect the living conditions at school. The food rationing was getting to the point of two meals a day instead of three squares a day. Our room of cadets decided to send out a person to scavenge for extra food every few days to increase our food supply. Some nights, we might have some eggs or a chicken or some doves, and often nothing would come of a night excursion. The cadet who came back empty-handed was considered a Yankee sympathizer and shamed, so we all tried our best to bring back something. When my turn came up, Sam looked at me and said he was starving. "Bring back something tasty, Pat, please."

As the others told me, I would look good in blue if I didn't. Willie offered to go with me, but everyone thought that the more people that went out, the more chance of being discovered outside the school. Local farmers were already complaining to the commandant of missing livestock, eggs, and even pies set out to cool in the evenings. Pies were the best. So off I went, sneaking out the window and climbing down the side of the building. Since I knew the path the walking guards took, I could easily slip through the grounds without being seen. Once I got outside of the school, I was in darkness. The good thing I did was every day, I had time to go out and see what was around and near the school. I noticed some farms around that raised pigs. I didn't want to get into a pig fight, so that farm was out. Cows were too big to handle, so those farms were out. I knew of a farm (Mr. Simms's farm) that raised chickens mainly, and he allowed them to roam about in a big pen far from his house. That was the place to go. But first, I visited some of the window sills of local houses just to see if any pies were out cooling. No luck there, as they didn't seem to be leaving pies out like they used to. I made my way over to Mr. Simms's farm. Mr. Simms would often come to the school to sell his chickens, and he would love to talk with the cadets. He had a son fighting in the war and was very proud of him. I knew he wouldn't mind if I took a few of his chickens to help feed the future soldiers of the Confederate Army.

On the farm I was raised on, I had experience raising chickens. I knew they were very noisy when disturbed, and I did not want to wake up Mr. Simms, or I could be the first cadet killed in the war. My plan was simple: draw some chickens to the edge of the pen away from the group and hit them with a stick. I used my famous chicken call to lure in a couple of chickens, but all the chickens came over just a clucking. What a ruckus and a light came on in the house. Out came Mr. Simms with his old musket blunderbuss. I knew that gun had only one shot, but it was probably full of lead pellets that made it hard to miss its target. I stayed perfectly still as Mr. Simms walked around looking at his chickens. I didn't know why, but chicken feathers had always tickled my nose, and I felt a sneeze coming on. I grabbed my nose and clamped down with my fingers hard. Whew, the urge went away until I let go of my nose, and the loudest sneeze erupted. Mr. Simms jumped back and hollered, "Who's there? I have a gun, so show yourself."

What to do? Can I just run? No, he is right on me now. "Don't shoot, Mr. Simms. It is just me, Cadet Pat Morgan."

"What in tarnation are you doing out here after midnight? Are you fixing to steal my chickens?"

"Mr. Simms, I am terribly ashamed as I was contemplating doing just that. But only a couple. You see, the school meals are not what they used to be, and we need to eat to keep up our strength. The cadets need to be strong when General Lee calls on us to help him fight those damn Yankees. You know they are coming this way."

"I heard that," Mr. Simms said. "How close are they?"

"Pretty close, and you know they know we are here, and they will stay away from here because of us, so we must be strong, and food is needed."

Mr. Simms thought about it for a while and put his gun down. "You know, Pat, if I give you these chickens, everybody will be here stealing my chickens."

WHERE ARE MY FRIENDS AND FAMILY?

"Well," I agreed with him, "that would be a problem for you. How about I tell my roommates that I found these two chickens in the woods running around free? I first went to your farm, but you had two huge dogs guarding the chicken pen, and I was nearly killed by the dogs."

Mr. Simms seemed to like that story as he smiled. He said, "Well, that sounds pretty good. I tell you what, you can have two chickens if you can catch them."

"Yes, sir, that sounds fair." Over the little fence I jumped. I chased those chickens for twenty minutes to the delight of Mr. Simms, who was enjoying my difficulties. I had enough of this. I picked up a big rock and heaved it into the chicken mob, and down went a chicken. Right in the head. I picked up another rock and threw a fastball into the mob, and down went another. I popped them both right in the head, but to make sure they were done in good order, I popped them once more in the head. Mr. Simms was amazed at my rock-throwing. He said, "Now you have your chickens, so go on back before you get caught."

"Mr. Simms, thank you, and the Confederate Army thanks you."

"Go on, get back to school."

I put the chickens in my satchel, and off I went, happy as I could be. But before I headed back to the school, I had to check a few window sills for a pie. No luck. A couple of pecks on the window and all the gang was there to see what I brought or to embarrass me for being empty-handed. Sam, Robert, Henry, and Willie were ecstatic at what I had scavenged. Sam looked in the satchel and pulled out the two birds and noticed that the heads were slightly damaged. He asked if I mugged them as, by the looks of them, they must have put up a good fight. We plucked the birds that morning and cooked them up with some butter bread. The breakfast that morning in old room 45 (number of our room), I assure you, was not at all objectionable, and I think from experience that the old saying is true, "Stolen things always eat the sweetest."

It had been bitter cold this winter at school, and doing early morning drills and pulling guard duty at night had caused me to fail quite a bit. But I had been suffering through these difficulties. A letter just arrived from my pa. This always excited everyone in our room, as we like to have the letters read out loud. Willie, Henry, and I knew a lot of the same people back home.

This was the actual letter from Joseph B. Morgan to his son Patrick on February 13, 1863.

> We have just heard that the guerillas had attacked the enemy in Pasquotank killing Tom Cox and probably some others. We hear that the Captain, commanding in Elizabeth City, has ordered all the people White and Black to report to him, and it is said he intends to compel them to take up arms. This whole country is in a perfect ferment. The people are growing desperate and the inhuman treatment of our enemies seems to be driving every man capable of bearing arms into the bushes or into the army. How long such a state of things is to exist, the Lord can only determine.
>
> My health is very bad right now. I am suffering among other things with a sore throat and have been for some time past. The rest of the family are well.
>
> I should be glad to hear from you. Not one word yet since Albert left have we heard from you. Mrs. Shaw gets letters from Willie and Julian and I should suppose yours could come in the same way. Send them to Col. Shaw and he will forward them if you will request him to do so I am sure. Ma sends her love and says she would like to write, but you must not think because she does not, she has forgotten you. Other causes prevents. I have hastily penned these few lines this morning having just heard of an opportunity

for sending a letter out. Your uncle James is still with us and talks of coming out soon.

Your Father
Jos B. Morgan

Willie and I were very sad to hear about Tom Cox. He stayed home to help his pa run the farm, but I guess he got fed up with the Yankees looting and stealing from his pa and decided to join the guerillas. I wish he could have come with us to VMI. A lot of my friends were scattered around as they were either staying on the farm to help their families survive, in which case they had sworn allegiance to the Yankees or taken up with the Yankee army or run off and joined the Confederate Army. These are tough choices to make and choices you never thought you would have to make. Surely, this war would end soon, or there would be nothing left for man or beast.

My pa was not happy I had not written recently. I had to tell William Shaw (Willie) and Henry Wood to stop writing to their folks as much as it made me look bad. But free time at school was such a luxury, but I knew I should write, and I would write a note tomorrow. I would tell him about the boring goings-on here at school. I made short work of my letter starting on March 23, 1863. It was a day set apart by the Confederate States as a day of humiliation, fasting, and prayer, and of course, we were compelled to attend church (the Presbyterian as usual). The day being very muddy and sloppy, there was an unusual display of legs by the young ladies of the seminary, which resulted in several unappreciated remarks from the cadet bystanders. This week was bright and sunny, but still it was wet and sloppy. Notwithstanding, we had an inspection and marched to church in ranks. The Rev. Mr. White reproved the cadets for their past conduct. I had seen pamphlets floating around barracks concerning the maltreatment of ex-Cadet Daniels while here and also the proceedings of the legislature about the affair. They had ordered the officers of the institute to take measures to find out the names of the cadets who participated in the bucking and dismiss them immediately. There were some troubled cadets here who needed to be thrown out. "He is right about there being troubled cadets here, Pa. But don't worry about me, as I have Willie to protect me."

Commenced snowing last night and continues to do so at a rapid rate. Thrown on guard duty after taps, only walked forty-five minutes for my whole tour, and amused myself running after rats (four-legged ones, that is). That was the sum of my letter. I would only add to my letter that we commenced with trigonometry today, and we got served pork for dinner. Something I would not say in my letter was that Old Spex brought out an order this afternoon forbidding us from wearing our overcoats from this date until further orders. Also, that shawls and clothes and all articles not prescribed by the regulations should be removed from the cadet quarters and placed in the arsenal. Of course, the next day was the most unseasonable weather I ever saw, with snow coming down and no heat in the barracks at all. I didn't want to worry my pa and ma about my well-being.

I just got a note from a friend in Hertford, North Carolina, on March 29, 1863.

This was an actual letter written to Patrick from a friend, WH Cowell (cousin), dated February 15, 1863.

> Dear Pat,
>
> I have just come through the lines and have with a letter for you which I will mail at Weldon. Write me immediately on the reception of this and I may be able to carry it through to your father on my return. Tom Hampkins and myself are going to Raleigh with a lunatic. Then I am going to Greensboro, Lincolnton and Charlotte. Bill (Dozier) is married to Miss Barnard. Mr. Wiggington is dead and there is much sickness in Currituck. The Yankees are carrying on high in Elizabeth City. They have nearly driven all the citizens away from Elizabeth City now and then killing one. They murdered George Fearing last

thursday. They have destroyed the salt works on the Banks and excuse this bad writing. I am in a hurry and have a miserably pen. Give my regards to Will Shaw and Mr. Wood. Tell them that both their families are well. I was at Dr. Woods a few days ago. Write and direct your letter to my care Weldon.

Yours in friendship
WH Colwell

I wondered who the lunatic was that got Tom and William to Raleigh. I daresay it probably took a lunatic to try to get through all the Yankees checkpoints, but I was sure glad they made it. Willie and Henry were glad their families were doing well.

The war was destroying my home, and I couldn't do anything as I was stuck here. Some of the other cadets had tried to get kicked out of school. The most impressive cadet had to be Jaqueline Beverly Stanard, who, according to the rumor, had accumulated over a hundred demerits and was still in school. I heard he left for a short period of time but had since returned. I knew all we could do was hope we got a chance to fight because I knew we were prepared well for battle.

Lately, I have become very ill as I couldn't get this cough and fever to go away. I went to the infirmary, but the medicine wouldn't cure me. I got a demerit for wearing my overcoat on the post after taps. When you get a demerit, you have to write a written excuse to the commandant. My written excuse was (actual excuse as written) the following:

> A chilly night, and I felt very uncomfortable without an overcoat as I was unwell. I thought it very imprudent to be without it.
>
> Respectfully submitted by Cadet Morgan
> To Commandant of Cadets

That was my second demerit actually as I got one earlier when this ailment began. Absent from morning drills on April 15, 1863.
My written explanation was the following:

> It was raining and disagreeable morning, and my shoes, being very inferior, were also having a cold. I thought it very imprudent for me to go, as it would make me worse.
>
> Respectable submitted by Cadet Morgan, PH
> Note my use of the word imprudent. Very impressive, don't you think?
> To Commandant of Cadets

The cold persisted longer, and I could not get relief. I had to spend some days in the infirmary. When I got out, I immediately got my third demerit.
My third violation occurred on May 8, 1863.

> Visiting on the eighth of May 1863
>
> My explanation: I had just come out of hospital and could not find any of my books in my room. They had been misplaced during my absence. Some of my roommates told me that someone in room 34 had borrowed them. I went to go get them, and while doing so, I was reported.
>
> Respectfully submitted by Cadet Morgan, PH
> To Commandant of Cadets

I still could not get over the effects of this terrible cold when the cadets were called out to attend the funeral of General Paxton.
My fourth violation was being absent from drill on May 12, 1863.

WHERE ARE MY FRIENDS AND FAMILY?

My excuse was the following:

> When I had come from the funeral of General Paxton, the day was very warm, and having marched nearly three miles, I was taken with a very severe headache, which compelled me to take my bed and rendered me entirely unfit to attend to the above duty. At the time of the sick call, I reported to the surgeon and got some medicine.
>
> Respectively submitted by Cadet Morgan, PH
> To Surgeon VMI

Fortunately, I got over that nasty cold and got back to my duties and studies. Talking about studies, I've never had harder classwork. If it wasn't for mathematics, I would be a total loser. French, English, composition, Latin—all were very tough.

On Tuesday, May 7, 1863, the mail this morning brought bad news—namely that General Jackson was severely wounded in the left arm. It is feared it would have to be amputated and that General Paxton was killed and also Captain Davidson. All were from this town. General Paxton's and Captain Davidson's bodies were to be brought up to the institute and to be buried here. On May 9, Captain Davidson arrived and was lying in the society of Cadets Hall. On Saturday afternoon, the Corps attended his funeral underarms and had to march in the middle of the street with mud up to our ankles. On May 12, General Paxton's remains arrived last night. They were brought to barracks and would be interred this afternoon, Tuesday afternoon. The corps escorted General Paxton's body out to his house (only three miles), and there brought him back again to the cemetery where he was interred with the highest military honors.

On Monday, May 11, the death of our lamented hero, "Stonewall" Jackson, was announced. This was a terrible blow to the South. The news of his death reached us last night at midnight. His military career filled the brightest and most momentous pages of the history of our country and the achievements of our army. He departed this life at Guinea Station last Sunday at three fifteen o'clock. His remains would be carried to Richmond, where they would be in a state for one day, and then brought here in Lexington for interment. On May 13, all academic duties were suspended today in honor of the old hero. On May 14, General Jackson's body arrived by boat at one o'clock, was escorted to the barracks by the Corps, and placed in his old section room, which was draped in mourning for the period of six months. He was in a fine metal coffin. The first flag made in the South of the new design covered his coffin. On the flag were wreaths of evergreens and flowers. It was the request of his wife that he should be buried tomorrow, Friday, May 15.

Guns had been firing at half-hour intervals all morning in honor of the lamented Jackson. The procession formed in front of the Sally port at half past ten and commenced to move at eleven. Corps were in front of the caisson on which he was born. Then a company of cavalry and, after that, a company composed of all wounded and all that were once members of the old Stonewall Brigade. Bells were tolling all over town. The funeral sermon was preached by the Rev. Dr. White.

The good news was we were now mostly drilling and learning war tactics. Normal classwork had been greatly reduced, but there were times when I was so worn out from the constant drilling that I missed the normal classwork. Just to sit in a chair for two hours and listen to a citation would be a nice break. I was very interested in artillery science. I was told by my professors that I was a natural with angles and measures of distance. We drilled on the canons about three times a week, which allowed me to miss a marching drill. That was a nice break, as those muskets weigh ten pounds, and I knew that toting them around was difficult. Our artillery unit had two (three inches) rifled guns and two (3 inches) guns. Each battery (or cannon) was pulled by four to six horses. It took about six cadets to man each gun. I found out that organizing and positioning a single cannon for firing could be a confusing task. When we set up before a battle, we followed an orderly step-by-step procedure. But when we had to move fast to a different position, it was all chaos. We practiced

WHERE ARE MY FRIENDS AND FAMILY?

over and over the process of quick movement, trying to simulate movement as in battle. It was difficult when time was not critical, let alone doing it in trying circumstances like battle. The next thing we learned was preparing to fire the canon. Each time, load, fire, and reload had several steps, and each step was repeated exactly the same way. This ensured no accidents would occur during battle when all hell was breaking loose. We could do these steps in our sleep. The men in each group learned all parts of the procedures. This was in case someone fell during battle, someone in the group could take his place. A plus for me in the artillery was that horseback riding was a must. Fortunately, I was a very well-accomplished horseman, if I don't say so myself. Being able to deal with horses was very important, as without horses, we couldn't move our guns or ammo. The first thing a Yankee would shoot were the horses, as he knew he could cause the movement of the artillery to be slowed or stopped. But I still had to do some long squad drill marches.

I was able to return home in August for ten days. I got my furlough due to keeping my demerits below ten for the half year (most difficult thing I did this year.) I saw my two brothers, Francis, who was fifteen years old, and Joseph, who was two years old. My sisters, Lucy (fourteen years old), Lydia (ten years old), and Ida (seven years old). They had all grown so much, and baby Joseph was talking a little. I spent a lot of time being spoiled by Ma, who kept me full of food and loved me every minute. All of my friends were gone, and the farm was in need as all of our Negroes had run off. Most of them went to join up with the Yankee army. I imagine Fred probably joined up with the Northern armies. That's one future Yankee I hope not to meet on the battlefield. Some lived off the land as best they could, and if they couldn't find anything to eat, they stole to survive. Some roving bands of Negroes would plunder at will, settle old scores, and terrorize the farmers.

The crops were ready to be harvested, and there was no help to be found in the county. I helped Pa all I could, but I had to return to school. I explained to Pa that I should stay on the farm as he needed help, but Pa insisted I return to school. Everything had changed, and not for the better. The enemy made raids upon us and plundered and destroyed our property. Disease was ever present, carried by hordes of soldiers and sailors passing through crowded encampments. The diphtheria had been very prevalent. My ma had been doctoring the local people for diphtheria and had been suffering one debilitating illness after another. I wish she would stay away from the sick, but she insisted that Dr. Cowell couldn't do it all and that the sick needed caring.

I returned back to school without much trouble from the Yankees. The drilling and marching had increased as war was coming to the Shenandoah Valley, which was toward the Virginia Military Institute. How can we not get into the fight now? It was coming to us.

I was glad to get an hour's rest to relax in my room. I had just laid my head down when a messenger brought me a letter and said, "This is for Cadet Patrick Morgan. Is he around?"

"Yes," I said. "That's me." It was a letter from my pa.

It was dated October 11, 1863.

> My dear son,
>
> I have been intending to write you for the last two or three weeks and indeed ever since the reception of your letter advising us of your safe arrival at Lexington. We were very glad to learn that you arrived there safely and in good health. We heard after you left of the raid of the Yankees in the upper counties and were fearful you might have some difficulty in getting along though I can scarcely believe they would have prevented you from going to school. Since you left the cavalry have been pretty thick among us. They are quartered at Currituck (Court House) and make frequent excursions in search of guerrillas. They had a skirmish with them the other day. I have heard in Camden near Major Gregory in which they say the Yankees had two killed and 3 or 4 wounded.

WHERE ARE MY FRIENDS AND FAMILY?

There has been a protracted meeting at Sawyers creek. About twenty persons were received Baptised. On Sunday the last day of the meeting about twelve o'clock the cavalry from C.H (Currituck Court House) made a dash up to the church while Mr. Overly was in the midst of his sermon. They called out the congregation and formed the men in a line in the road in front of the church and examined every man. They were in search of guerrillas. Fortunately there was none there. They carried off two Confederate soldiers who happened to be at the meeting. Monday morning Baptism took place at the float bridge and just after the congregation had dispersed the cavalry from South Mills dashed up. They were in search of Dorsey Sanderlin Jr. who no doubt had been reported to them. He was one of the members Baptised in the morning. I understand he was at dinner in his father's house. He ran out of the back door and made his escape. The Yankees are said to have fired 11 shots at him.

Since you left Sam and Charles have gone to the Yankees at the CourtHouse and if they remain I expect the remainder will leave soon.

I have not regained my health though I am going about. I have fevers every evening and it seems almost impossible for me to get well. The rest of the family are well and I trust will remain so. We have had much sickness in our family this fall. Much more than common. Your Aunt Julia is still sick. She has another son and I hope will soon be better. Ab is reading medicine with Dr. Cowell.

I believe I have given you all the local news. The war news You know much better than I can inform you. We get very few southern papers.

The last I have seen was the 25 Sept. Your Ma and children and all send their love. Write often as you must know it affords us much pleasure to hear from you. May God bless and protect you my dear son.

Your Father

Oh boy, I'm glad Dorsey got away from those Yankees. Eleven shots were fired at him, and not a nick on his body. He was lucky it wasn't Johnny Reb shooting at him, or he would have been full of holes. I heard now the Yanks have repeating rifles, which made up for their poor marksmanship. A Reb only needs one shot to take down one Yank.

I was sorry to hear that Sam and Charles went to the Yankees. They were good men. I would hate to meet them in combat on the battlefield, but they were the enemy now and would be dealt with as such. The one thing I did not miss was those protracted church meetings at Sawyer Creek. They lasted all morning, and Mr. Overly could preach without taking a breath of air for two hours. But prayers were needed to end this war and get these damn Yankees out of our lands. I hope the good Mr. Overly was in good standing with the Lord and had his ear.

Today, the academy had a visit from General Thomas Lafayette Rosser. His brigade had wintered only a mile from Lexington, and before departing for the spring campaign, General Rosser had come to the institute and presented a captured flag to the corps of cadets. We accepted the flag politely, but many of us took this gesture as mocking the corps for its lack of experience in battle. Willie spoke for all of us. We didn't want other regiments going out and capturing our flags for us.

"I agree with you, Willie. Just give us a chance. We'll capture some flags on our own. Ever wonder what it would be like fighting Yankees?" I said.

Willie said, "My pa said it was the best feeling ever."

WHERE ARE MY FRIENDS AND FAMILY?

Some of the cadets whose fathers were generals and officers chimed in by saying, "There is nothing like it."

"I was thinking the opportunity is coming soon, boys. I hope we will be ready."

The actual letter was dated January 3, 1864.

> My Dear Son,
>
> It's been a long time since we have had a letter from you and we are beginning to feel very anxious to hear from you. I wrote you a short time since giving a short statement of our troubles and devastations and excitement produced by a Brigade of negroe troops under General Wild passing through our country. But it is utterly impossible for me to give you anything like a correct idea of the state of things in our midst. I have just returned home from Fortress Monroe. The citizens of our country held a meeting and appointed Dr. Colwell, A.J.Lowe, B.L.Dey, B.M. Baxter and myself, a committee proceeded to Old Point, headquarters of General Butler, who is in command of the Department of Va. and N.C., for the purpose of ascertaining what was required of the peaceful inhabitants to secure their property from destruction and their dwellings from the flames. We left last Sunday and passed through their lines by way of Deep Creek. Col. Deforest in command at North West treated us very courteously and gave us a passport to Gen. Getty's headquarters, which is some three miles back of Portsmouth. We had a very pleasant interview with Gen. Getty, who seems to be a perfect gentleman and who kindly facilitated our business by giving us a passport and transportation to Gen. Butler's headquarters.

Tuesday morning at 8 O'clock we took the boat for Old Point, where we arrived about ten AM. We obtained an interview with Butler about three o'clock, PM. He received us very respectfully and treated us very courteously, and after hearing our statement conversed with us some half an hour or more very pleasantly. He said nothing was required of us only to remain peaceful and use our influence to put down guerrillaing and blockade running; that being accomplished we should not be further molested by his troops; that he did not include us in his General Order No. 49, nor did he consider us within his lines.

We returned home and reported the result of our interview with Gen. Butler. We had hardly got home when a squad was sent out to enroll the habitants of Camden and Currituck. We are inclined to believe, however, they are recalled, and we may be allowed a short respite.

Your Ma has been quite ill but is now fast recovering. Jodie is suffering from croup very much. All the rest are tolerable well. I am not very well but hope am improving.

Everything is excitement and suspenseful and God only knows how we get along. All is gloom and doubt around us, but God governs in the affairs of men and will bring all things right in the end. Your Ma is trying to get some shirts ready for you, and whenever we can procure anything for you, will send them by the first opportunity. Some of my friends talk of going to Richmond and if they do I shall try to send my horse by them with instructions to sell him and you the money. It may come when you do not need it and if so take care of it for future use. You must be economical and make the best use

WHERE ARE MY FRIENDS AND FAMILY?

you can of both time and money. Should they bring him out, I shall instruct them to sell him and have the money insured and sent by express to you. All send their love and best wishes, and I pray that a kind Providence may preserve and protect you, my dear son.

Your Father J.B.M.

PS. Since writing the enclosed letter, your two letters of the 13th and 27th of december have come to hand. We are glad to learn you are so well after your exposure and hope you will not suffer any serious consequences. All are well here and send their love. Those gentlemen I spoke of coming out have returned. They sold my horse for $600 and I trust you have recd the money.

J.B.M.

Let me tell you that money came in handy as I needed new shoes and socks. The weather was harsh, and I was suffering from exposure, but I never missed a drill or class. But with a new long john, I would be much cozier while marching or, better yet, on those long guard duty nights. Thanks, Pa, for all you do. I will make you proud as you have made me proud by telling those Yankees to stop bothering the regular folks. I am surprised that General Butler was a gentleman to my pa and his committee. I mentioned the name of General Butler, and I got a different opinion of him from my teachers. They told me that General Butler was the commander of the Department of North Carolina and that he was a dumpy, bald-headed, sour-faced state senator from Massachusetts whose political savvy propelled him to high command. He even voted for Jefferson Davis to be the Democratic candidate for president in 1860. Imagine that, he voted for old Jefferson himself. Among the Confederates here, he was referred to as "the beast." It is said he rules with an iron hand, as he did in New Orleans. I hope Pa's committee could trust him to do what he said he would do and call off his soldiers from messing with the local folk. For many inhabitants, the last straw was the raising of US Colored Troops from locally freed slaves. I hope my best friend Fred from Pa's farm was not one of them. A local Black leader, Abraham Galloway, recruited the local freed slaves and called them the first North Carolina Colored Volunteers. As I understand it, these Negroes volunteers only patrolled the local areas. I am sure this caused much concern for the past slave owners to be policed by their old slaves. A lot of revenge could be gotten. The world was turned upside down.

Every day was the same as we drilled and took more tactical war classes. Several of our professors had been killed or wounded in battle.

We knew that the manpower of the Southern army was being stretched to its breaking point. The cadets had been sent out at different times to help drill new recruits, and we had a very fine reputation for drilling these recruits, but we wished to do battle, not drill raw recruits. Cadets had been called out to stand in reserve during small skirmishes. We never were a part of any fighting, returning each time from these missions dejected as we were to stand ready or guard the wagons behind the battle lines, never getting into the action.

One of my saddest days came by letter as Willie received a letter from his ma today. The letter told how his father was killed in battle at Batchellor Creek, near New Bern, on February 1, 1864. The commander of his brigade stated the casualties were small in number, but the loss of Colonel Shaw was deeply deplored. I know of no one filling a similar station whose loss would inflict a greater injury to the service than that sustained in his fall. Willie was overwhelmed with grief, and even though his father was a very strict man and treated Willie like a soldier and expected him to be tough, Willie loved and respected his pa. He was his hero. All of Currituck respected this man, and we know we lost a community leader. A letter came later telling of how the Yankees stopped Colonel Shaw's funeral in mid-service. A list was made of those in attendance. This is how much he was respected by the Yankees. Colonel Shaw was at the battle of Roanoke. His commander was General Wise. General Wise was very sick during the battle; this left Colonel Shaw in charge. Colonel Shaw's troops had to retreat, and he was captured. He was released a few months later and continued as a Confederate officer till his death. His death was the last straw for Willie as he was packing to desert and join up to avenge his father. I kept telling him we would fight the enemy soon and wait till summer, and if we did not get into battle, I would desert with him. Everyone in the room agreed to desert with us. This calmed him down, and he agreed to wait until summer.

The days drag by with some classwork but mostly drilling and war tactics. We, in artillery, had been able to fire the cannons, although we used about a third of the powder we would use in battle. We had four cannons that were specially made for VMI. Slightly lighter and smaller than the typical cannon of that type. A specially designed custom smaller carriage. The reason we needed a smaller, lighter cannon was we had no horses to pull the cannons, so we had to pull them around using cadet force only. Almost every horse in the area that could pull a wagon was taken for the war effort. Only sloped back hags were left for the townspeople. These cannons were a little smaller, but they carried a huge boom. The noise could burst an eardrum if you don't back away from the cannon when fired. These four cannons were christened: (the four apostles) Matthew, Mark, Luke, and John. Named by Colonel William Nelson Pendleton and the seminary students. They named the guns the four apostles because they spoke a powerful language. We learned early on how powerful they were, as we always have balls of cotton in our ears during firing practice. We learned early on not to touch the cannon after firing, as poor Cadet Davis was ordered to put his thumb over the vent of the cannon while loading it. He screamed in pain as the cannon barrel was very hot, and as he ran around looking for a bail of water to stick his hand in, Captain Minge used him as an example to the rest of us. The captain informed us to always wear the thumbstall over our thumb as the barrel may be extremely hot. Cadet Davis would have a badly burned thumb for a while but would never forget that lesson.

James Reid was the best cadet we had in artillery, but he left the academy early this spring to report to the Thirteenth Battalion, Virginia Light-Artillery, Company A. We were very proud of him. All the cadets were, but particularly the artillery guys. If he could fight, then so could we, as we learned the same gunmanship as he did. It felt like we would get into war sooner than later. We had to.

I missed my friends from home. It was good to have Henry, Sam, Robert, and Willie here at school with me. A lot of friends we left behind, and I wondered what they were doing and where they might be. I had written some letters to friends, but I didn't know where to send them. I kept the letters so that when I found an address to where they were, I could send them immediately. Sounds silly, but it did my heart good to express my feelings on paper, and I hoped all the letters got into the hands they were meant someday, for two reasons: this means they are still alive, and they can see how much I really care for them.

The cadets continued to try to keep warm and find enough food to keep our strength up for the constant drilling. I hoped my family had a beautiful Christmas dinner. I wrote them a letter about my Christmas dinner by saying as compared to their dinner, I was confident when I gave them a bill of fare of the one which I had the pleasure of masticating, they would not, for one moment, hesitate in saying mine was still more beautiful. First, we had a cold loaf of bread (not enough for sixteen loaves) and also warm corn bread. Second, cold beef. For dessert, molasses, water, etc. Oh! Indeed, I feared if I went on and enumerated the rest, I would not finish this letter soon. So I left it for you to form an idea. My mouth ran water whenever I thought about the dinner I missed. Why couldn't I have been there?

Christmas was the dullest Christmas I had ever spent. Only one day were the classes and drilling suspended. A few boys got tight(drunk) owing to the scarcity and high price of liquor. I slept most of the time to rid myself of the monotony in my room. We were all hoping for a package from home to bring us some joy. Unfortunately, the packages were brought to us by way of a packet boat, but it had not made its appearance as yet, and judging from the looks of the river, which I could plainly see from my window and which was entirely frozen over, it would not be so for some time to come. We had almost despaired. The first thing we would all say in the morning and the last, I believe, at night would be, wonder if the boat had come! I think we spent at least most of our time in the day standing looking, in vain, down the river. The one good thing about a frozen river was you could go skating, and today, I could not avoid the temptation. It was really elegant fun. You could go down the river as far as you wished. There were also a great many ladies on the ice who seemed, evidently, to think there was more fun in falling down than standing up, but unfortunately, in the height of their enjoyment, one of them (frisky) fell rather too hard and almost broke her nose. Poor girl. I guess it would spoil her beauty spot, and I knew it would teach her a lesson on how to run on ice again. The fall of this unfortunate lady, of course, intimidated and somewhat marred the pleasure of the remainder of the party, and there was no boat in sight with our care packages.

Finally, a package arrived from Ma. It was a nice box of eatables, and I assure you, I enjoyed them no little and did justice to the box, as well as my roommates, who said that it was the best that had been received in room 45 (my room). We played fearful havoc with the turkey pies and cakes. Nothing now remained, I am sorry to say, but my ham which I hoped to enjoy for some days yet as it was a fine one. I sat down and wrote Ma a letter.

> My dear precious ma,
>
> Where did you get the turkey from? I did not think there was such a thing left in the county of Currituck. Why did you not keep it and also the ham? I had much rather you should have done so, for I know how scarce such things are with you since you have had the army among you so long. You ought not to have deprived yourself of it. I can manage to make out with the beef they give me here, although it makes me sick about once a month. I have been feasting on Robin

pie lately. Willie and Sam went out hunting and brought back nineteen birds. I was able to get the judge (the school's cook) to cook them up for us. I believe half the corps were out yesterday looking to shoot some birds, but all had bad luck, frightening every bird away for ten miles around.

> Your loving son,
> Cadet Patrick Morgan

Frustrated by our lack of opportunities to fight, we had a meeting of the student body in the early part of 1864 and voted to offer our services to fight General Lee himself. Lee was obviously impressed and responded that he appreciated our gesture but that he preferred that we stay in Lexington. He did give us some hope by saying he would call on us if he saw a need. That gave us hope that maybe he would need us, so we continued to drill and march, hoping one day, that need would come, and he would call us to battle. We needed to hold on to something as the life of a cadet was more difficult. It was cold, the food was awful, and they were drilling us to death. The new cadets (rats) coming in were the greenest rats I had ever seen; no sense at all. They were no older than fifteen or sixteen years old. I guess all the older boys have been conscripted into the regular army.

I just received a letter from my cousin John B. Wiginton, dated March 12, 1864. The letter was sent to me from Camp Gatlin Murfreesboro.

> Your letter of the 26 of February came to hand yesterday and found me well except weakness. I have just returned from Camden. I had a sick furlough and it happened in a good time the confederates went down just behind me and placed their pickets at (Shingle Landing). You may depend that I had a gay time, we had a party at Mr. J. Ambros Dozier's, we danced nearly all night. I danced the first set with cousin Archibelle, the

second with Maggie Fanshaw. Mr. Ambrose Dozier also danced, we had three members of the church on the floor at once. I went to see Henry, (Willie's brother). I stopped by your house a day or two, they were all well I believe. I went to see my (Mattie) twice while I was there and found her as lovely as ever. She is a perfect angel and as precious as a diamond. I went to school with her both times, walked with her alone to the academy and spoke of the past, present, and future. Jesse Williams has gone in on furlough this morning. I wrote to Mattie and sent yours enclosed to the institute. Marcus (Travells) was on furlough the same time I was, he came out with me, we had fine times together. Try and get a leave of absence and come see me. Mary sends her respects to you and says she would be pleased to see you if you would write me when you think you can get one. I will manage to get one the same time, and we will go in together.

I have not time to write much more as I have to make out requisitions for rations for the men this evening. Our company are all in Camden except eight and they are without shoes consequently neither they nor I have but little duty to perform. We manage to draw rations enough for ourselves and cook and eat. If I have accused you wrongfully I beg your pardon. You spoke of my flirting with my intended much sooner would I destroy my own life. What deceive my first and only love and the best girl that ever graced the side of this gentleman. Do not speak of it again you will make me tremble to think of such a vile thing. You speak of being low spirited, you must cheer up and if you will do your duty I think you will be able to accomplish all you wish for.

I have made Mat promise to use her influence in your behalf and you know she can be of much use to you. I had a letter from a young lady in Petersburg yesterday. She thinks I am a flirt, little does she think that I am engaged but I will not deceive her any longer for I respect her very highly. I will ask to be excused and to be her friend in the future and not a lover. Our regiment will start over the river tomorrow morning. I have had the men that are with me belonging to our Company excused from this march, they seem to be very much pleased at it. We will have the whole camp to ourselves. I wish you were with me so that we could lay in our bunk and talk of our sweet hearts. I hope the time is not far distant when we will be able to go where we please, then we can visit our sweet hearts and not be looking for the infernal yankees to come and capture us.

I also had a letter from brother Isaac, he is well and in Petersburg. I believe all of our friends and relatives are well. Write soon and tell Wood to write to me. Give my respects to all of my inquiring friends, if any and reserve a greater portion for yourself.

Your cousin,
John B. Wigginton

Sounds like old Jesse had a good visit home. I'm a bit jealous though, as Jessy joined up, and I was sitting here in school. I'm very jealous he got home and saw his girl and danced the night away. I could only imagine how great that must have been. But he was serving his country, and I was stuck at the academy. Mr. Dozier always threw a great party. If you could get the elders of the church to dance in public, then that was a sign of a great party.

WHERE ARE MY FRIENDS AND FAMILY?

John was a great flirt, and he knew better than to step out on his girl, but he drew the line apparently with the lady in Petersburg, and now he was still an honest young man. I did miss Mary and hoped my letters were getting through to her. I would also like to be free to go where I please without fear an infernal Yankee patrol would capture me. It was good to hear my family was doing well and that John was able to visit them and spend time with them.

We were on the eve of freezing up. It had been one week since we had a particle of heat (there not being a stick of wood at the VMI). What a change had taken place in the weather. Today, it was snowing hard, and a cold wind was blowing, and still we had the same duties to attend to, both academic and military. It was outrageous for the boys. We couldn't study a bit. It was so cold we could not stand it any longer, so we called the roommates and went out and made a raid on Old Spex laths (woodpile) and built up some sort of fire and all gathered around like a gang of chickens under its mother's wing. If the officers of the day should, by chance, visit our room and catch us, we would get a hard report and a few demerits. I believe I was sure even the officers of the day were in their rooms trying to stay warm.

Word was General Spex got a letter a few days ago from a gentleman over toward Hot Springs, who had, I believe, been in General Averil's camp (Yankee) and said Averil was preparing to make a raid in this direction. He advised General Specs to fortify all the mountain passes, which he planned to do. Two cadets were sent out to make a survey. I suppose we would have to build the fortifications ourselves. Is this what I came here for? To shovel with a spade and dig with a hoe? If so, I think I would ask Pa to just as well give me his consent, at once, to my resigning and entering the regular army. I wanted to have some of the glory of the trenches in the year '64 attached to my name, and this war couldn't last much longer. It was so cold I had to stop worrying about the war and try to stay warm. I had to lend some of my roommates' money so they could buy something to eat. I was able to do this with the money my pa sent to me from the sale of the horse. The school was starving us out now. We got half a loaf of bread and miserable rye coffee without milk or sugar. It had caused an eruption to break out on a good many of the cadets. I believe this place had become a prison. For the last two weeks, they had been giving us nothing but rotten beef. The bad news was Old Spex had fifty or sixty barrels of it put away and would keep feeding us on it, old scamp! He had about ten or eleven barrels of molasses and wouldn't give us any. I think we would riot if we had the strength, but with all the drilling, there was no energy left but to jump into bed to get warm.

I expected by July, the cadets would be taken into service out in the mountains. I had heard rumors to that effect. I wrote this letter to my pa and ma.

> Dear Pa,
>
> I believe my experience here at VMI has matured me to become a man, a soldier. People may not know my age, and, of course, they will not tell you they thought I ought to be in the army. I believe the government will take the cadets into the army by July into the mountains. I prefer being with Lee. Ma, I don't want to desert or be shipped out against your will; therefore, I beg that you write me a permission note to resign so I can use it at my own discretion. Whether I will or not, I am not sure yet. If you give your consent, then mention that it is concerned with family matters that prevent you from sending me here any longer. Ma, I hope you will not let what I have written distress you. You should be more firm and patriotic and want me to be in the army. I know this is not a natural desire to send your child to war by any mother. Ma, I must go as the mail will be taken up soon, so I shall bring my letter to a close, and now darling mother, with love to all the family and oceans to your sweet self, I must bid you good evening, hoping what I

have written will not cause you trouble and that I will soon hear from you.

> I am, as ever, your darling boy,
> Patrick (May 9, 1864)

I am in want of draws…

PS. Today was a very warm day, and I had to attend a drill for two hours. We had two charges 100 yards across the parade ground on a pretend breastworks. It was very exciting the first time as I was second to get onto the dreaded breastworks. The second time was not as thrilling as I was fourth to reach the breastworks. I had to leave the ranks at the dress parade because of a violent headache and faint feeling. But I am now rested and feeling all right and ready for another row. The drum is beating for a tattoo (roll call), so I must close.

Tomorrow was a special day, May 10, 1864. There would be a suspension of academic duties in order to raise the flag sent from Europe over the grave of our lamented leader, Jackson. This day off after the raising of the flag would be a welcome time to rest. The drilling and hot weather had been exhausting, and I was looking forward to some nap time.

I missed mail pickup yesterday, so I would include today's events (May 10, 1864), the first anniversary of Stonewall Jackson's death. We played a significant role in the ceremony, with a cadet honor guard chosen to raise the flag over Stonewall's grave. The ceremony was short but impressive, and we, the cadets, were very proud to be a part of it. After the ceremonies were complete, we were given the rest of the day free. Pa and Ma, it was quite a day. Love to all, your son Patrick.

That night after the ceremony and in my free time, I was resting comfortably when I heard a drum. Henry and Sam were excitedly insisting I wake up. As I came to my senses, I realized the drum was a long roll, a call to assemble; something big was happening. In my mind, I remembered the past calls to assemble. A fire, last time. Or maybe we'd be sent out to guard a baggage train while the real soldiers get to do some fighting. I thought I better get going and catch up with my roommates. As I ran to the parade ground, I heard a lot of cadets grumbling out loud.

Once outside on the parade ground, we all were excitedly hoping that this was it. We were being called out to defend our country in battle. There were several officers standing near the statue of Washington. One was holding a lantern over his head while the others were using the light to read the paper the officer was holding. Suddenly, the first sergeant, in a very loud voice for the wee hours of the night, yelled out, "Fall in, A Company!"

We quickly fell in and snapped to attention. One by one, the commands were given to B, C, and D companies, all responding as they should. The role was called, and as the last name was called, Adjutant Weston stepped forward with the paper in hand. He cleared his throat and, without much ado, said, "I have a dispatch from General Breckinridge to read to ya'll. It read, 'Sigel is moving up the valley. Was in Strasburg last night. I cannot tell yet whether this is his destination. I would be glad to have your assistance at once with the cadets and the section of artillery. Bring all the forage and rations you can. Have the reserves of Rockbridge ready, and let them send for arms and ammunition if they cannot be supplied at Lexington.' This dispatch is signed by Maj. General John Breakinridge."

My heart was pounding so hard I could hardly hear the words. The next words out of Weston's mouth caused some concern to every cadet. "It will be necessary to keep some of you here at the institute to serve as guards."

Every cadet's, including mine, heart dropped as no one wanted to be left behind. Weston continued on, "The first sergeants and Captain Minge will detail who will serve as artillerists from each company."

WHERE ARE MY FRIENDS AND FAMILY?

Please pick me! I thought, or did I say that out loud? No, nobody turned to look my way, so I guess not. *Pick me. Pick me.*

Major Ship stepped up to say a few words to us as he would be leading us into battle if we got the opportunity to fight.

"This is an opportunity you all have been waiting for. I know you will give a good account of yourselves if you are called on to go into battle. You have prepared well. Now it is up to you to show what you have learned. We will be marching at daybreak, and we have been ordered to report to General Breckinridge at Staunton. You will take sufficient rations for two days' march. We will replenish supplies along the way. Now you have much to do and not much time to do it. Prepare well and try to get some sleep. You have a long march in the morning." The adjutant announced, "Parade…dismissed!"

A loud hooray was heard as we could not hold in our excitement. The cadets might have an opportunity to go to war, but some were not coming with us as they were chosen for guard duty. These thirty or forty cadets would be left at the institution to protect the school and the sick or injured cadets that were in the infirmary. Much crying and cursing was heard, but we that were going had no time to console these cadets as we had to prepare for the long march to Staunton. The first sergeants then picked eight cadets from each company to serve as artillerists. I was selected as one, and after I knew where I would be, I headed for the infirmary to tell Willie (Shaw) the good news for me and break the bad news to him. He did look pretty sickly as I walked into his infirmary room. I asked, "How ya doing, Willie?"

He sat up in bed and said, "What's going on out there?"

I told him, "General Breckinridge has just called out the cadets. The Yankees are coming to the valley. The best news I've heard yet. Let me get my pants on. Some cadets will have to stay at the school to guard it. I feel bad for them, but they have to do their duty. Willie, your name was called out as one of the cadets who will be staying at the institute."

"No goddamn way am I staying here. I've been stuck here at this school, and now I finally get a chance to kill some Yankees."

"I know, Willie, but you are sick, and there is no way you can keep up with the army marching eighteen to twenty-five miles a day. I'm so sorry, but I have to get all my stuff ready, for we leave at 7 a.m."

Captain Collier Minge (who was nineteen years old and was the highest-ranking cadet) would be in charge of the artillery. Lieutenants Fredrick Claybrook and Levi Welsh would be in charge of the type of ammunition to be fired and aiming the guns. Corporals Otis Glazebrook and Patrick Henry would be the gunners and would be the ones who give the commands to fire the guns during the action. The rest of us toted the ammo and prepared the guns for firing. One of my jobs was to drive one of the horse-driven ammo wagons where they needed to be as we followed our infantry in the battle.

Each of us would carry an eight-pound rifle (1851 Cadet Springfield musket), five pounds of food (for three days), blanket, water(canteen), bayonet, and forty rounds of ammunition. After I gathered all I needed, I needed a rest, so several of us just sat around and wondered if this would be the time we get to fight the Yankees. I decided to write a note to my folks as I knew this letter would not get to them until well after the battle.

Dear Pa and Ma,

As I write this letter, we are preparing to march to Staunton to assist Maj. General Breckinridge. It is possible we will be in a battle, and I am so very glad to finally have the opportunity to fight (maybe) for my country and for you. I am sure I will be safe, but if not, know that I am a willing soldier who fought for his country. Do not be sad, but be proud of your son, as I am proud to be your son. My goal is to make you proud. I only pray for you to be safe and that I can see y'all once again.

Your loving boy,
PH Morgan

WHERE ARE MY FRIENDS AND FAMILY?

All artillery personnel came with me. Captain Minge had called us together to prepare for the march. He explained we had been unable to gather a sufficient number of horses on such short notice, and we couldn't immediately take the artillery pieces along. This would delay the artillery's departure by a few hours. However, we would still be going. Whew, a sigh of relief was almost audible as we realized we were still going. This gave us some time to get together and talk about our part, possibly in a battle. I knew the guys from my company A well. I trusted them. The first cadet I was surprised to see in our group was Lewis Davis. He looked like he was twelve years old. I hadn't seen him much since he scorched his thumb on the cannon. I hoped he brought his thumbstall with him. His thumb still looked scarred up good. He was only fifteen years old. George Seaborn, William Hayes, Peter Temple, and the oldest and most respected James Larrick, who was twenty-five years old, were all in my company A. I was glad to see them. Our Lieutenants Fredrick Claybrook and Levi Welch stepped up to tell us what they expected of some of us. They emphasized that they would be in charge of what munitions to be fired and where to aim the fire. They announced the cadets who would be the carriers of munitions back and forth to the guns. Then Corporals Otis Glazebrook and Patrick Henry would be the gunners who fired the cannons. Then they proceeded to select the cadets who would prepare the cannons before and after the firing. Me and a few more were to be responsible for the wagons and horses. When it was time to move the cannons, we needed to hook up the horses to the wagons and the cannons to the wagons. I was given the job of driving one of the caissons. This was great as each caisson had six horses to pull it. I was thrilled to get this job. Driving a team of six horses would be an experience.

Our group was also to fill in for anyone who was injured in battle. Damn, this was serious business. It was stressed to all of us that we must protect the horses as the Yankees would be gunning for them. Without horses, we could not move the cannons. Captain Minge reminded us that once the battle began, we would be firing the cannons every two minutes (rapid fire), and the movements of the artillery would be quick and efficient. He expected our cadet artillery squad to keep up with the other veteran artillery squads in rapid fire and movements of the cannons. Now stay close as we would be leaving as soon as the horses arrived.

Meanwhile, the sun was about to rise, and the cadet infantry was in formation to begin their march to Staunton. Major Shipp spoke to the cadets, "You boys are all aware of the proud traditions that have been established here at the VMI. Many brave men have gone before you, graduating to take their places on the fields of battle. They have made the entire South proud as well as this fine institution. Today, you are being called on to continue that proud tradition. We don't know if you will be called on to fight, but if you are, I trust that you will all do your duties. Remember what you have been taught. Remember where you are from. Remember what you have been trained to do. And do it well."

Shipp ordered musicians to take your positions!

At Shipp's signal, the drums began the march cadence, and the fife joined in. The cadets were stepping out!

A loud cheer rose from the ranks as one voice. Those who were staying bravely choked back tears. I could not believe the comments made by some of the cadets marching off to war.

"We'll tell the Yanks y'all said hello!" yelled one cadet. This caused some laughter from the other cadets.

"Keep the Yankees out of my room!" shouted another. The mocking shouts rang out for as long as the cadets could see their ill-fated friends.

Meanwhile, we had a lot of work to do once the horses arrived. The VMI artillery consisted of two three-inch rifled cannons. One cannon in a battery used two six-horse teams. One six-horse team pulled the cannon with its limber (a two-wheeled carriage with an ammunition chest on it.)

The other six-horse team would pull a limber attached to a caisson (a caisson was a larger two-wheeled carriage). The caisson had two ammunition chests and a spare wheel on it. These carriages were made of oakwood, very strong and very heavy. Each horse pulled about 700 pounds. We needed twenty-four horses. We came up with twenty-four horses. Not too bad, considering we only had six hours to find them. That was a lot of horses to maintain. The good news about that was we could ride the horses on our march to Staunton and catch up with the rest of the core by midafternoon. Fortunately, we did not have the chests completely loaded down with ammo as we would be supplied in Staunton so everyone could ride a horse on the march.

There were twenty-three cadets in our artillery battery. Our ages ranged between fifteen and twenty-five years of age. The youngest cadet's name was Lewis Davis. He was the youngest cadet that was called out. Corporal Henry and I were not sure about little Lewis being able to pull his weight in battle, so we decided to give him a test. We called him out to carry some bombs to the caisson. We told him not to move too fast as these particular bombs had not been made safe to travel, but he needed to carry them to the bomb deactivation room. Once the deactivation was done, then he could load them into the caisson.

"Why me?" Cadet Davis said.

"Well, why not you?" I replied. "You cannot do your duty to get us ready for a battle. Are you scared?"

The corporal looked at me and said, "I told you, Pat, he was not going to be of any use to us."

Well, that got cadet Davis peeved. "I can do any job as well as any cadet here."

Corporal Henry said, "Well, go on then."

Every cadet was aware of poor Louis carrying high explosives to this deactivation room, so they all lined up along his path. Cadet George Seaborne was the first one to see him with a bomb.

"Whoa, young man, do you know you are carrying a live bomb?"

"Yes, I was instructed by Corporal Henry and Cadet Morgan to take the bomb to the deactivation room."

"Good lord, man, we don't have a deactivation room," George said, trying to maintain a straight face. "I want you to stand tall right where you are until I speak to the captain. Do not move one muscle. Do you understand, Cadet Davis?"

"Yes, sir."

At this time, all the cadets nearby scattered, leaving Cadet Davis alone with his bomb. After about fifteen minutes, some cadets came up to him and began to accidentally bump into him. Cadet Davis was screaming to leave him as he had a live bomb. This went on until poor Cadet Davis could no longer hold the bomb as it was a twenty-five-pound bomb. He screamed for help, "Please, someone take this bomb. I can no longer hold it, and if I drop it, it will blow the school up."

I, along with all the rest of our artillery battery, came to his rescue. I stepped up to take the bomb from him. As I was getting a good grip on the bomb, it began to slip from my hands. As I was losing my grip, I flipped it over to Cadet Seaborne, who threw it over to Cadet Temple, and around it went till all the cadets had a hand on it at one time. Cadet Davis was white as a ghost as he ran to fetch his bomb from us.

He kept saying, "You're going to kill us all." Just as he got to the last cadet who had the bomb, just about within Cadet Davis's reach, the bomb was thrown up into the air. All the cadets took off in a rush, screaming, "It's gonna blow!" except Cadet Davis, who made a tremendous effort to catch the bomb, but the bomb hit the ground in a cloud of dust. He missed it. He fell down and covered his ears, waiting for sure death by explosion. All he heard was laughter from his fellow cadets.

Corporal Henry and I helped Cadet Davis to his feet. With a tear in his eye, he said, "Sir, I tried to get that bomb to the deactivation room." This brought the rest of the cadets to tears from laughing. "You guys could have blown up the school, you bunch of fools!" Cadet Davis yelled.

I leaned in next to his ear and quietly said, "Cadet Davis, we are very impressed with your call-to-duty attitude, but this bomb has no fuse in it and is completely safe to drop-kick all around this courtyard."

"What you say!"

Second Lieutenant Welch came over and congratulated Cadet Davis for his determination to do his duty even in the face of death.

WHERE ARE MY FRIENDS AND FAMILY?

"All you cadets should respect this man, for when an order is given, I hope all of you will do your duty as well as this young lad has done."

It was strange, but after we saw how determined little Cadet Davis acted, we were impressed. I myself believed he would be an excellent artillerist, and he showed that he was strong as he held that cannonball of twenty-five pounds for more than an hour. Everyone apologized and shook his hand.

"Cadet Davis, you are all right," I said.

Everybody pulled together to load up the limbers and caissons. Since we did not have to carry a lot of munitions, we instead filled the free space with food rations. My job was to pick the strongest twenty-four horses who would pull the cannons and wagons. Then I hooked the horses up to the cannons and carriages. By noon, we were able to begin our march toward Staunton. The sun was out, and the day was perfect for a march. Captain Minge believed we should meet up with the infantry by nightfall. The great thing about artillery was we got to ride on the horses and carriages since the load on the horses was about 40 percent. What a pleasant march this would be. We all were in good spirits as we crossed the old wooden bridge over Woods Creek near the edge of the institute campus. After a couple of hours, the heat of the sun was becoming a problem. Every chance, we stopped at a creek so the horses could drink. We could only imagine what the other cadets who were on foot must have been feeling. I was riding in the back of the wagons, and the dust was suffocating.

Since I was in charge of the horses, I rode up to Captain Minge and told him I noticed a slight limp in one of the horses up at the front wagon. I suggested that maybe I should ride beside this beast to monitor his gait. Captain Minge agreed (Whew) and ordered Private Peter Temple to change positions with me. The smell of fresh air (dust-free) was delightful.

As we were getting close to our corps, young Private Lewis heard a rumble and, without thinking, said out loud, "Is that artillery?" That caused some laughter from the ranks.

George said, "Sounds like lightning to me."

A few minutes later, the rain began. By the time we arrived at our camp, the thunder was rolling, and the rain was pouring. The corps was back together in camp, and it was miserable. I was so sore from being on horseback I could not sit on my butt. There was no dry spot to sit in anyway. The next morning, after sleeping off and on through the rainy night, I quickly realized I was not at school anymore. Colonel Gilham (Old Spex) allowed us a short time to cook and eat breakfast, and then he ordered us to rank once more the artillery falling in behind the last row of Company D. I was so wet from the rain as my uniform just absorbed the moisture. It felt like I was carrying ten extra pounds. But, of course, I was riding a horse, and I had it much better than the poor souls who were on foot. One good thing about the rain was the dust was gone, and since the artillery was in the back of the column, it made the march much better for me. The road became mostly mud. The rain kept falling, and it was a slosh through on that second day. The only good part of the day was we passed by homes and farms, and the people rushed out to wave and shout words of encouragement. I liked the children who marched with us for as long as they could. They had sticks for guns. It made the march seem shorter, and this raised everybody's spirit. I was happy that the people greeted us as soldiers who were fighting for their freedoms. The kids who followed us with pretend stick guns were yelling, "Kill Yankees!" These Yankees were not long ago our fellow Americans, friends, family, and government. Both sides were teaching their children to hate the other side. It hit me right then that this war was not going to end until one side was destroyed. The hatred from both sides was so extreme that I wondered if we could be a single country ever again.

    Ad nauseam came over me, and the rain continued to fall. By midmorning, I saw real soldiers for the first time. They were off the road. I never saw a more exhausted group of men just spread all about the side of the road. I thought to myself that these were real men who had been in battle and survived. But my admiration quickly decreased when I heard one old soldier ask if my mommy knew where I was and if she had made those cute clothes for me. Some of the soldiers laughed at us. I was about to respond in a juvenile way when Captain Wise said, "Keep marching, boys. Eyes front.

WHERE ARE MY FRIENDS AND FAMILY?

I think we may not be welcomed by the older soldiers. I don't think they believe we will fight. We will show them if we get the chance."

"Staunton, two miles!" Commander Ship called out.

A loud cheer rose up from the corps. At last, we were at Staunton, and I had plans with the boys. There were several all-girl schools in town, and I had my sights on meeting as many as I could. As we marched toward the town, I saw several companies of soldiers camped beside the pike road. Once again, we were hounded with many slanders.

One old veteran shouted out, "Where you fine soldiers from with those nice uniforms?"

Several of us proudly answered, "Virginia Military Institute."

Another man shouted out, "That's a girl's school, isn't it?" That drew a laugh from his friends. "Welcome to Staunton, girls!"

I was tired of marching even though I was on a horse for most of the march. I had had enough insults from this group of old soldiers, so I asked the group of soldiers, as I would regret later, "Why are you sitting on your asses when the Yankees are invading our valley?" Whoa, I made a mistake 'cause those are fighting words.

Fortunately, Commander Shipp took command of the situation, ordering the corps to remain silent and continue marching. Whew, I was about to start a battle right then. At that time, Commander Shipp shot me a look. I immediately wanted to hide. Further down the road, we approached a group of soldiers who looked like they had been fighting the war since day one. They were nice and sang to us (out of tune, by the way) "Rock-a-Bye Baby" at the top of their voices. The corps and I held our anger in check and remained quiet, marching straight to the tune of "The Girl I Left behind Me." Everyone was exhausted after our two-day march, and we were energized by the song. Shipp saw an open area off the pike and called a halt and directed us to set up camp.

Before he dismissed the troop, he stood before us and spoke, "You boys did well today, and I'm proud of all of you." He continued, "You didn't say a word to those soldiers that were making fun of you (maybe one cadet did say a word or two back), and I know how hard that was. It was hard for me too. But y'all did good. Believe it or not, they're on our side, and if you get called to fight, they'll fight as hard as any soldier ever fought. So don't think too harshly of them. They're just having their fun. If all goes well, we'll get our chance to show them how a VMI cadet can fight."

I wish I could have insulted them old vets better than they did us, but I had to admit, those insults were pretty good.

Shipp continued on, "Now there's a lot going on here, with all these troops in town, and it ain't all good. So just to make sure we don't have any problems, I'm gonna have to restrict everyone to camp while we're in Staunton."

This was terrible as I wanted to see Staunton and maybe a few young ladies also. The whole corps went silent with this news. Nothing to do now except make camp and take care of the horses. But I knew Cadets Carrington Taylor, Jack Stanard, John Wise, and Louis Wise had planned to visit Cadet Taylor's home and have a nice dry home-cooked dinner in a nice dry house. I was sorry they were restricted to camp and jealous as I was not invited.

We set up camp and tried to keep our fires going as the rain continued to pour down. There was not a dry place anywhere. I was fortunate as I could lay out under the wagons. It was still wet but much better than most had it. While I was making myself comfy, I could make out four figures coming toward my bedroom (wagon).

"Well," I said, "where you fellas heading to on such an awful evening?"

That startled them except for Cadet Stanard, who immediately asked in a very soft voice, "Who the hell wants to know?"

"Hey, Jack, it's me, Cadet Pat. I just saw you passing by, and I wondered where you were off to."

"None of your business," Jack said.

"I believe it is my duty as a cadet of VMI to report you disobeying an order restricting you to camp." I knew they were going to Cadet Taylor's house for a nice home-cooked meal. "Now I could be persuaded to look the other way if, say, you bring back some food for me, as I know y'all are heading to Cadet Taylor's house for a fine dinner."

"You wouldn't turn in a fellow cadet," said Cadet Taylor.

"For some good fried chicken and fixings and cake for dessert, I'll turn my ma in."

"No way am I bringing you jackshit," said Stanard.

Cadet Louis Wise, who was the youngest cadet, decided maybe he wouldn't take the chance of getting caught. His brother, Cadet John Wise, also started to waver, and I could see I might get a good meal out of this meeting.

"All right, Pat, we promise to bring you some food."

As they raced off, I reminded them, "Don't forget dessert!" I crawled back under my wagon, praying they would make it into town and back with my home-cooked meal. My mouth watered just thinking about it.

I felt a tug on my leg that woke me from a deep sleep. It was Stanard with a sack full of food. He tossed it into my abode (wagon) and said, "Choke on it."

I said, "Thank you, and your secret's safe with me." Best late-night dinner I ever had.

Come morning, I was soaked to the skin, but my belly was full, and I was ready for battle.

We learned this morning that we would continue to march down the valley. This was disheartening as we had hoped to stay in Staunton for a day or two to rest. Also, Staunton was the home of several girls' schools, and many cadets wanted to meet the young ladies, hoping, as soldiers now, the ladies would be more apt to notice them.

Shipp was instructed by General Breakinridge directly that he wanted the cadets to march to Harrisonburg, our third straight day of marching. The rain was still falling, and the roads were turning into mud. The cadet corps fell in behind Echol's brigade, and another day of marching began. May 13 started like the other days as we marched in the rain and mud, but as we came close to Harrisburg, we began to see the signs of war, and several times, we had to stop on the side of the road to allow travelers to pass. These people were fleeing the Yankee advance into the valley. I asked one old man where he was going.

He said, "I'm going anywhere there ain't no fighting going on. No damn Yankee will be having any of my stuff as this here wagon is loaded with everything I own, and boy, I hear that Yankee army has fifteen thousand men marching down the valley." He shouted, "God bless all you, boys!" as he went on down the pike. Soon there came all kinds of wagons and carriages full of people with all their belongings. This was a sight I was not prepared for, but this sight made me feel pissed off. How dare these Yankees force our people out of their homes. It was a pitiful sight, and I wanted to help my people, but lo and behold, the horse manure filled the road and mixed with the rain. Once we got back on the road, we walked through mud and horseshit for a mile or two, and then the rest of the livestock came. Farmers were driving their cattle, pigs, sheep, and even ducks and geese. As we stepped aside off the road to let these poor homeless families go on by, we looked down the road behind them. I could actually see shit floating in the middle of the road. Once all the beasts and birds passed by, the cadets stepped back onto the road and sloshed our way onward through the rain and mud and animal increment (shit!). I saw one cadet throw up, but the captain told us to hold our noses and continue to march. I never expected the horrendous smell we had to march through, but the cadets, to our credit, continued onward. Several times, we passed groups of farmers herding their livestock, and we stepped aside so they could pass. Onward, we marched into the rain, mud, and manure. The life of a soldier was no picnic. It was not as glamorous as I thought it would be.

By midmorning, we saw our first group of wounded soldiers. They were covered in mud, and as we got closer, I could see that some were missing an arm and others a leg. This sight I would remember for the rest of my life. Battle was not for the weak of hearts. I saw that most of the cadets and I averted our eyes when the wounded passed. After another mile, Captain Shipp ordered us to halt and take a spell. Not more than twenty yards away, Echol's brigade was also taking a rest. The older veterans were talking among themselves and paying us no mind. I was glad because every time we met up with our older comrades in arms, they usually made bad jokes and ridiculed us. It felt good to rest. I felt some guilt because I was on horseback for

WHERE ARE MY FRIENDS AND FAMILY?

most of the march, one advantage of being an artillerist. We have wagons and horses to ride on as the foot soldiers have only their feet and their shoes. We all have the same type of shoe, and they are not that comfortable even for parade marching on a beautiful day, let alone sloshing through rain and mud. We are marching twenty to twenty-five miles a day in mud and animal waste. Some of my friends took off their shoes and hid them in their packs, hoping when the rain stopped, they would have a dry pair of shoes. But so far, the rain had not stopped, so we should see how that worked for them. I think that idea would prove to be all wet as their packs were getting drenched as well. Everything was drenched with this constant rain. The only thing I'd seen was several cadets limping from stepping on sharp objects on the roads that were hidden by the puddles of water. By the end of the march that day, I believe everybody had their shoes back on.

Mr. Shipp ordered us to take a break, and we pulled off the muddy road and slumped down on the wet grass, exhausted. I saw this old soldier sitting on the wet ground nearby. His clothes were soaked from the never-ending rain. He caught my eye and asked me, "Hey, boy, you ain't never seen a real live soldier before?"

I immediately turned my head the other way to avoid any confrontation.

"I'm talking to you, boy," he said as he began to move toward me.

Oh shit. I thought I might be in for a beating. I don't want to have my first taste of battle with my fellow soldier. I felt my fellow cadets tense up, and that assured me that I wasn't alone here. Even one of the boys (Cadet Wise), whom I blackmailed into bringing me a home-cooked meal last night, I could feel behind me. Cadet Wise was tapping my back to let me know he was there. Apparently, the old soldier saw my anxiety as he approached me and said, "Don't be scared, boy. Nobody here is going to hurt you. I just wanted to know if you have ever seen a real soldier before." :

"No, sir, I can't say I have seen a soldier who has actually fought in battle."

He said, "Well, here I am," as he did a little twirl for me to see every bit of him. "Nothing but an ordinary man just like you except a little bit older."

I added to his description of himself under my breath, "A little bit odorous also."

A soldier nearby must have heard and chimed in, "That's a sure fact."

I realized that these men meant no harm, and we (cadets) began to ask the men questions. The first question shot out of Cadet Davis, who was the youngest cadet in our corps, "Y'all ever seen a real Yankee?"

I was embarrassed. What a childish question to ask an old soldier. Yet I was kinda interested in knowing myself.

The man answered, "More than I care to remember, son."

"What are they like? Are they good fighters?" Cadet Davis asked.

The old soldier said, "The ones I've seen ain't no slouches as they fought purty good."

"They good shots?" Cadet Stanard queried.

That made all the old soldiers lift up their heads with that question.

"Not as good as we are!" the corporal said. "Them Yankees are best at foraging."

This brought an amen from the other soldiers. The corporal continued, "Anytime we follow the Yanks through an area, there is no food left to be found. I swear they even take the bark off the trees."

A soldier with a beard down to his chest said, "We speak the king's English. I hear tell no two men speak the same language. To be in command, you have to speak German, Dutch, Irish, French, jest name it."

"I heard that myself personally," offered a sergeant.

The questions were flowing between the two groups as Shipp gave the command to fall back into ranks.

"You boys take care," the soldier said.

I said, "Thank you, sir. It was a pleasure meeting you all, and God be with you."

The march was starting again.

WHERE ARE MY FRIENDS AND FAMILY?

The artillery marched along at the end of the line. Most of us jumped on a horse or carriage, so we did not mind the actual marching. But as time went by, the smell of the animal droppings was so bad that we put our handkerchiefs around our nose and mouth to breathe. The fleeing residents increased as we marched closer to Harrisonburg. Often we had to jump off the road to avoid crashing into a wagon or carriage or running over a chicken, cow, goat, etc. The march was getting to the corps, so I decided we needed to get our minds off of this monotonous march. I decided it was time to play a joke on poor Cadet Lewis. He was the youngest and the most vulnerable cadet around, and he was riding on a horse, looking as happy as a lark. I told Cadet Lewis his horse looked like it was limping, and he needed to walk to give the horse a break. Lewis was not about to get off the horse and walk in the mud and poop, so he refused.

"Cadet Lewis," I said, "I am in charge of the care and safety of these most valuable animals, and I order you to get off that horse. If you do not obey my order, I will relieve you of your duty and send you home." I'm not sure I could do that, but he sure got off that horse. He slid off that horse right onto a cow pie. As he was scraping off the cow pie from his shoes, he had to dive into the gully to avoid being run over by a fleeing carriage. When he crawled back up to the road, he was covered in mud, poop, and drenched. Everybody got a kick out of the show. As he approached me, I said, "Cadet Lewis, as I look at that horse, he appears to be walking normally. It must have been the slippery road conditions that made him look unsteady. You may climb back on him if you wish."

To my surprise, Cadet Lewis smartly gave me a salute and got back in the saddle. All of us were surprised as the laughter stopped. Again, Cadet Lewis impressed his fellow cadets. He might be the youngest, but he was gaining respect as time went by.

We arrived just outside Harrisonburg and set up camp in a little clearing in the woods. We were so drenched by the nonstopping rain that the first thing we did was make a fire to dry off and get warm. We settled next to our fires after dinner for a well-deserved rest, but as we were getting cozy, wherever we could find a dry spot, the sound of wagons and horses was drawing near. Several of us got up to see what was coming down the road.

To our amazement, a Confederate cavalry detail was coming down the pike. They had Yankee prisoners with them. I called to the other boys, "Come see this. Real Yankees."

This brought several cadets out of their dry spaces to see real live Yankees.

Corporal Henry turned to the other cadets and said, "All of you who thought Yankees were eight feet tall, take a good look. They are no different from us. They are men just like you."

"Well," I said, "they do look like us, but they can't shoot or fight as good."

This brought a cheer from the cadets. After they passed by, we all went back to our wet beds and slept as much as we could that night because we knew that another long march was starting early in the morning. We prayed the rain would stop because, for sure, we couldn't get any wetter.

It was Saturday morning, May 14, 1864, and just like the last three days, we were on the march. The rain was still falling, and even though our uniforms looked the best as anybody's, they were showing the signs of a hard march in an unrelenting rain. I think my uniform weighed fifteen pounds more than it did when I started this march. But I had to give credit to those cadets who were not in artillery as they had to walk. The corps has lost at least three cadets I know of from illness, and they were left in Staunton. They were heartbroken. They would miss the glory of battle. But I'm sure they won't miss marching through rain and animal shit. The rest of the corps wished all this marching would stop.

I thought, *Will we ever meet the enemy? Surely, the Yankee, Sigel, who is German, is somewhere close. We have to run into him sometime, as Virginia isn't that big. I am tired of playing soldier. We need a battle, anything, as long as we don't have to march. It's been three days of marching through mud, animal shit, and rain. I learned about a Bible story in school. It was about the forty-day flood that flooded the world. Maybe we should be looking for the ark and forget this war.* Crazy thought, but I was about to go crazy. It was like water torture, drop by drop, hitting you constantly on your head. Add to that, the roads were muddy, full of animal shit and water puddles. My skin was wrinkled from being wet everywhere, and this uniform would never be dry again, nor would it ever smell human again. Everybody was in a foul mood. The joy of being a real soldier had been gone for a while now. Ah, but the food in camp tonight was the target of the anger of most cadets.

I was sitting by the campfire, and Cadet Temple walked over to show me what dinner looked like. He held up a piece of meat, I think.

I said, "Pete, what the hell is that?"

Pete said, "That, my fellow cadet, is a raw piece of pork. You have a choice. You can eat it as is, or you can cook it and then eat it."

"I don't eat raw meat!" I said.

"Well then, I guess you'll have to cook it."

I took the piece of meat, stuck it on a stick, and shoved it into the fire. I mumbled to myself, "I didn't go to the institute to be no damn cook." I let it sizzle in the fire for a time as I walked around camp, seeing what the other cadets were eating. Satisfied that we all had the same raw pork, I went back to my little fire and pulled out my piece of pork. It was black and looked burnt. That was the best piece of meat I ever ate. Obviously, I was starving, so anything that didn't run away from me was going to be eaten.

That night, my stomach rumbled, and I passed a lot of gas, but I kept it down, unlike a lot of cadets who made several trips to the latrine to remove that piece of raw pork. It was an active night in camp. My reward for keeping my pork in my belly was guard duty. Shit. I was in no shape to sit up half the night as a corporal of the guard. Sounds impressive, but it only means you stay up most of the night to watch the moon. But not tonight. If you looked up, you would get a wet face as the rain was still falling. As I walked around guarding the camp from intruders, I could see my fellow cadets trying to sleep under wet blankets. I guess guard duty was not so bad if the alternative was sleeping in a puddle of water. I did my walk around camp and settled in next to the fire. I wrapped myself up in a blanket and sat. I passed the time thinking of home, family, and friends. I hoped I made them proud, as right now, I was not feeling as patriotic as I did three days ago. I could take a horse and ride out of here. Stop that kind of thinking, Pat. I heard a noise, someone coming toward me.

"Holy Mother of God, Stanard, I could have shot you!"

"Come on, Pat, your gun is lying next to you, and I'm sure it isn't even loaded. Who would give you a loaded gun anyway?"

"Maybe so," I said, "but what are you doing walking around the camp at this time of night in the rain?"

"I just can't seem to sleep," he said. "I have this bad feeling about tomorrow."

I thought to myself, *Then why don't you stand guard so I can sleep?* But something was different about him. He sounded very grim. One thing about Stanard, nothing ever seemed to bother him. He was as carefree a fella as you would ever meet. So I held my tongue. I asked him what was on his mind.

Standard sat down beside me, looked me right in the eye, and said, "I think I'm going to die tomorrow."

"That's crazy, Stanard." As I said those words, I turned toward him, and in amazement, I saw tears running down his cheeks. He continued, "Pat, I think I'm going to die in battle tomorrow."

"No way, you, of all people, are not gonna die in battle."

"Hell, we more than likely won't even get into the fight, just like the last eight marches we've been on, and never once did we get a chance to shoot a Yankee."

"You are being foolish, so stop thinking that way."

"Well, I hope you are right, but this picture of me lying dead on the battlefield just pops in my mind out of nowhere."

As he poked at the fire with a stick, I could see his concern, and I began to wonder myself if, indeed, fate was telling him to prepare for death. Holy shit, I'm scaring myself now. "Stanard," I said, "you have too much life left, and besides, you have to get back to the institution, as Old Specs still has some demerits to give you."

Stanard smiled at that, and I barely heard him say, "I pray you're right."

We sat by the fire while not saying anything, just enjoying the quiet company of one another. Finally, I told him he had to go back to camp and get some sleep before he was reported. He slowly got up and left, but not before shaking my hand and pulling me in for a hug. I got the terrible feeling that this might be the last time I saw my friend alive. Shivers went down my spine as I thought that fate may be real.

I got up and walked around the encampment with the rain falling down the back of my neck and the thought of Stanard's impending death on my mind. One thing was for sure, I would not worry about falling asleep on my watch as my mind was full of questions. What if we go to battle this time? Is fate telling Stanard that his time is up? Will I be killed in battle also? I decided to head back to the fire and my blanket. On this guard duty, I didn't have to worry about sleep overcoming me as I was as wide-eyed as I could be.

After a couple of hours, I was startled by hoofbeats on the turnpike. I gathered myself up and went to see who it was galloping into camp. "Corporal of the guard!" the man on the horse shouted.

I rushed over to him. The man was an aide to General Breckinridge, and he told me he had orders from the general for Commander Shipp. I ran as fast as I could to the location I remembered the commander was sleeping.

"Commander Shipp," I said as soldierly as I could, "you need to come with me."

We both ran to the rider.

"Commander Shipp," the man said.

"Yes, I am Commander Ship."

"Orders from General Breakinridge, sir," the rider said. "You are to bring the cadets north to New Market as quickly as you can. General Breckinridge will meet you there and explain."

Shipp replied, "We will leave immediately, sir. Rouse everyone." Commander Shipp turned to me and said, "Tell them to be ready to march at once. We'll assemble on the pike. Be sure to tell the cadets to be quiet. No drums or loud talking."

It didn't take much to rouse the cadets as they were ready to march into any battle. We had marched through mud and shit for four days, with rain falling every day with very little sleep. The cadets were ready quickly to finally get to battle and end this unbearable marching. Commander Shipp was upon his horse so every cadet could see him. We'd been given orders to move at once to New Market. He began, "There has been fighting going on in that area for several days, and I have been informed that General Breckinridge expects it to get worse. He wants everyone, including us, to get there as soon as we can. It looks like we may finally get our chance to show what a VMI cadet can do. If that happens, I have confidence that you will do your job well."

I felt butterflies in my stomach, and I would admit it: scared. Commander Shipp must have sensed the fear and the grimness in all of us.

"Before we leave, I think we should have a word of prayer," said Shipp. "Colonel Gilham, will you do us the honor?"

"I would be honored, Mr. Shipp. But I believe that this honor should go to Mr. Preston," he said, turning toward Mr. Preston.

Shipp said, "Would you, Frank?"

I said in a very low voice, "Why would they choose Mr. Preston to say the prayer?"

My buddy Peter, who apparently had an incredible hearing, nudged me rather severely and quietly whispered in my ear, "You dumbass, have you not noticed that Mr. Preston has one arm. He lost the other arm in battle. He should have the honor to say the prayer. Sometimes, Pat, I don't know how you walk and carry a rifle at the same time."

"Geez, Peter, I'm sorry."

"No, Pat, I'm sorry. I'm just a little nervous and tense. You're not a complete dumbass."

After the prayer was said, many cadets were wiping tears away from their faces.

"Nice prayer, Frank," said Mr. Shipp. Then turning to the cadets, he said, "Move out!"

The night was so dark on the pike that I almost trampled the cadets right in front of me with my horse. They were already angry about me on horseback, and they had to walk.

"Back that beast up before it tramples me."

WHERE ARE MY FRIENDS AND FAMILY?

It was so dark I couldn't see who said that, but I sure knew that voice. It was my roommate.

"Move your ass, Atwill. This battle isn't going to wait for you to arrive at your leisure."

"Who said that?" Atwill said. "I can't move any faster than the 255 cadets ahead of me, so keep your damn horse off my heels. It's hard enough marching through this mud and crap without you riding my ass!"

"Well," I said, "maybe I should just trample you to death and end your misery, Sam Atwell."

"I should have known it was you, Pat, back there enjoying your horse ride while we, simple soldiers, marched through this swamp of a road."

"Cadets, keep quiet! Yankees could be anywhere," said Captain Minge. "Pat, keep the horses, wagons, and guns further back behind the troops, and I do not want to hear anymore conversation."

"Yes, sir." Both Sam and I were quick to put our focus back on the march.

We marched silently through the night, and at first light, we were near our destination. Commander Shipp halted us and ordered the corps to stand off the side of the road. It was raining like never before. My god, will it ever stop?

Cadet Davis rode up to me, and he looked like a wet, whipped puppy dog. He quietly said, "If they are going to pray over us, maybe they think we're gonna get into a fight after all." He added this thought, "Y'know something else? This is Sunday, and all of Stonewall's big victories were on Sundays. Maybe that's a good sign."

I just nodded at him to reassure him, but I was surprised as it seemed to reassure me just a little bit. "Lewis," I suggested, "go get under the wagon before you catch pneumonia or something."

We stood there for two hours in the pouring rain. When the dawn brightened some, I could see flashes, followed by the roar of artillery. Has the fight already started?

When it was light, we started our march toward New Market and toward the sounds of guns. My stomach was full of butterflies as I thought, this time, I would see some action. I've never felt this kind of pure loathing and fear of the unknown. My excitement for the battle was waning with every step closer to New Market. Along the pike road, we marched past Wharton's brigade, which had stopped for a short rest. As we passed by, I heard, "Go get 'em, VMI!" But I knew we would get some gallows humor from the older men who had been in more than one battle. "Where do you get those fine uniforms?" said one old vet as he strolled along the cadets, asking who wanted him to cut off a lot of hair to send home to their mothers. That was a good one, I thought. The best one was yelled out by an old vet who had at least five teeth and a beard lying on his chest. He said, "You boys like rosewood or pine fer yer coffins?" Little did they know, we probably would never get near the fight.

Off on our march again, we arrived at milepost one and pulled off the road as a group of soldiers marched by, followed by a man on a magnificent horse. This man was tall in the saddle with a large mustache.

My captain said, "Behold, cadets!"

That there was General Breckinridge himself. I, along with every cadet, was so caught up in the excitement of seeing the general that we let out a cheer. General Breckinridge reined his horse and looked down at us. With a stern look, he said, "Boys, I admire your spirit, but you must be as quiet as possible. We are near the enemy. You must be cautious."

That got us back to the realization that we weren't at school anymore. We might have serious work to get to. The fear in my belly was back. As the general and his soldiers rode by, followed by the men under Wharton and Echol, we fell in behind the last man. I was on the final leg of my march to New Market. As we marched closer to the town, I could smell the rank smell of gunpowder, and then I could see the first houses of New Market. Commander Shipp ordered the cadets to follow Echol's troops up the hill to the left. Captain Minge ordered the artillery to go to the crest of the hill. The ground was very soft, and of course, it was still raining. Now the artillery had to get off our horses and wagons as the mud became thicker and pushed with the animals to free the wheels and push the cannons up the hill. Upon reaching the crest of the hill, Captain

Minge tried to maneuver the cannons into position, but the cadets were all standing in the way as if hypnotized by what they were seeing. From the top of the hill, they got a look at the enemy and the scale of this potential battle.

I yelled, "Clear a path for the guns! Let us through!"

The cadets snapped out of their fog and moved quickly out of the way. We were able to join the rest of the artillery on the crest of the hill (Shirley), professionally unlimber, and prepare to fire on the enemy. I was proud of our team as we were as professional as anyone else. All the cadets were observing us as we prepared to fire on the enemy. It was a thrilling moment for me. Corporal Henry aimed the guns on the cemetery down below, which had Yankee guns sprawled out among the tombstones. The moment came when Captain Minge ordered us to fire. The first cadet action in a battle occurred. When we fired our cannons, the cadets watching let out a loud cheer. We missed those cannons in the cemetery by a lot, but it didn't matter. We were shooting at the enemy. I turned toward my fellow cadets and waved and shouted.

It was odd that after we fired a volley, our guns remained silent as we sat in our position, not moving or firing at the enemy for two hours. I looked over at Lieutenant Claybrook. I asked, "Why are we not attacking?"

He just looked at me as if to say he wasn't calling the shots. Commander Shipp was ordered to move the artillery into a reserve position on Colonel Echol's right. As we moved out to join Colonel Echol's troops, our cannons had gotten stuck in the mud up to the axles. We could not budge them. Captain Minge was beside himself. No amount of cursing or yelling was working to free the cannons. Commander Shipp rode up to see why the cadet artillery was not keeping up with the rest of the corps. Mr. Minge explained that the mud was too thick to move the cannons. Mr. Minge knew if he could not keep up with the rest of the batteries, then he might miss the possibility of finally getting into the battle. We all knew if we did not get these cannons freed, we might miss our second chance to fire our cannons on the enemy. I did not want to miss my chance at firing that cannon again, so I was pulling hard on the reins of one horse.

The horse slipped and nearly fell on me. Mr. Shipp came riding up to Captain Minge with orders from General Breckinridge.

"Mr. Minge," said Shipp, "General Breckinridge has ordered the cadet artillery to report down to the pike and join Major McLaughlin's artillery immediately and tell him why I sent you." This was what Captain Minge wanted to hear. He had been ordered into battle. Eager to free his guns before Mr. Shipp changed his order, he rushed back to the stranded cannon and, with all of us working together, freed the last cannon. Soon we were speeding down the hill toward the pike. I was driving six horses with a carriage (loaded with ammo) with a cannon attached, and I have never experienced the excitement of racing down that hill at, I believe, the fastest I have ever gone. At the bottom of the hill, we turned left at a full gallop. The cadets still in reserve on the hill could see us and gave a loud cheer as they watched us rumble down the pike at full speed to join up with the main body of the artillery. Once we arrived at Colonel McLaughlin's artillery group, he advised us we would stay 200 to 300 yards from the battlefield and move forward as the battlefield moved forward. I was going to be in the battle. Oh my lord, what would my pa and ma say if they knew where I was? I have never been more alert and present in my life. I felt bad for the other cadets, who probably would be kept in reserve like every other time we were called out. But I would tell them how great it was. Should have been an artillerist boy.

For the first time in four days, the rain was beginning to lighten up, but no one noticed as the battle was about to start. I could hear my heartbeat so loud it hurt my head. Captain Minge ordered fire when ready. The artillery duels began. The noise, smoke, and smell were unlike anything I had ever seen or heard or smelled. Back at school, we only used a quarter of powder when we fired our cannons. The difference in noise and power was unbelievable. The smoke from one volley from our cannons completely blinded us from the field of battle. That did not stop us, as Captain Minge ordered a continuous fire, which meant fire as often as possible. We only adjusted our aim when the forward observer gave us a sign to aim more right or left, as we could not see anything in front of us. At first, the Yankee cannons firing back at us would cause us concern as we could hear the shells whistle over our heads. I could not stop ducking as they passed over, but I and the rest of the cadets soon focused on our job, shelling the enemy as often as we could.

Captain Minge ordered to limber up and advance into New Market proper on the south side of town. At the institute, we practiced this procedure of rapid movement of cannons. It was not an easy transition to limber and unlimber artillery. For our two cannons, it took eighteen cadets to accomplish it. Each cannon had a limber, which was a two-wheeled carriage. This carriage carried an ammunition chest and was attached to the cannon. It took six horses to pull the weight. In our artillery battery, we also had a caisson, which was a bigger two-wheeled carriage and often carried two ammunition chests with a spare wheel. These carriages were made of solid oakwood. So each gun in a battery used six horses to pull the weight of a cannon attached to a limber and six horses to pull each carriage. We had twenty-four horses in our gun battery. Six cadets were assigned to each cannon. Each cadet had a specific duty. I was responsible for getting the horses reined up and ready to receive the carriage. Private Seaborne and Private Temple's responsibility was to gather all ammo, place it back into the caisson, and hitch the cannon to the limber. The other three cadets helped whoever needed help. The last three cadets were responsible for protection. Every cadet knew each other's job in case a cadet was injured. I was proud of our group as we were almost as fast as the veterans in setting up and taking down our guns. I was particularly proud of Cadet Lewis, who, at fifteen years old, did his job well.

I could see the veterans were impressed with our ability, but no one said a word. Colonel McLaughlin ordered us to move out, and on a gallop, we headed to the south side of town. Once there, Colonel McLaughlin ordered everyone to unlimber and set up their guns to prepare to fire. I could not help but look over to the pike road after I had prepared my cannon. I could see my first dead bodies lying in contorted positions. I would not have known which side they were on if not for the blue uniforms. The people looked the same.

Captain Minge shouted, "Faster, boys, faster."

I quickly returned to my job. General Breckinridge came up to us, raised his sword, and shouted, "Give it to them, boys! Give it to 'em!"

We did our best for the general and fired on the Yankees for several minutes. Then artillery moved forward, and we cadets did our best to stay with them. As we moved through the town, I smelled a rotten pungent odor. This was mixed with the smell of gunpowder. There were bodies lying everywhere in the streets from the small battles over the last two days. The smells almost overwhelmed me as I felt like I might puke. We stopped on the northern side of town and set up our cannons. We were beside the cemetery. This is where the Yankees were when we first fired our cannons from the hill. Most of the tombstones were broken apart and displaced at odd angles. I guess we did hit our targets somewhat.

A mighty blast erupted down our line. Captain Minge looked at me with a grim look. Then he said, "Pat, go see if you can help anybody down the line. Cadet Davis, take Pat's spot."

I ran toward the fire and smoke. It was at the end of the battery. I could not believe what my eyes were telling me. Two cannons were blown apart, carriages splintered and crushed, the ammunition chests were exploding, and limbers tossed about. Several horses were wounded and kicking, trying to get back on their feet. The horses were kicking and dashing out the brains of men who were tangled in the harnesses, and cannoneers with pistols were crawling around the wreckage, shooting the struggling horses to save the lives of the wounded men trapped under the burning wreckage. I stood there stunned. Suddenly, I was handed a pistol. A voice said, "Get in there and shoot those damn horses before they kill any more wounded men." I looked to my left and saw a young boy trapped under a carriage that was burning, and two badly wounded horses were trying to get back on their feet, but the young man was almost under them and was in danger of being kicked to death. I ran to him. I tried to shoo the horses away, but they couldn't move, only kicking out in pain and fear. I love horses, but I had to shoot them both in order to get to the boy.

WHERE ARE MY FRIENDS AND FAMILY?

The boy couldn't have been any older than my cadet Lewis, but he was just as tough as Lewis. He jumped up, ready to return to action. He had a broken arm that was dangling downward toward his waist. I told him, "Boy, your gun is destroyed, and look at your arm. It's broken. I order you to go back to town and get some first aid."

He said, "Who are you?"

"I am Captain Minge, commander of the VMI artillery."

The boy stood at attention and, with his good arm, smartly saluted me. What a good soldier this young boy is. "Now get the hell out of here."

"Yes, sir." Off he went.

I prayed he made it to a medical area safely. I felt good as I was able to save a life, but the sound of cannons reminded me I was in a battle, and I had to get back to my fellow cadets. I got to my cannon group. We, as a group, were firing our cannons at a pace almost equal to the veteran cannoneers. The smoke and fog filled the sky. We could not see the targets we were shooting at. Captain Minge ordered us to continue firing in the general direction of the battle, hoping we were doing some good. *Will this rain ever stop?* I was thinking, *Will this battle ever end?* But just when I had time to think about where I was at or become scared, General Breckinridge came charging up to Captain Minge, giving him orders, but I could hear the man say, brandishing his saber with his horse prancing nervously, through all the sounds of battle, "Bring those guns up here where they can kill somebody!" I found a new source of energy, seeing our glorious leader asking us to bring the fight to the enemy. Even though we were exhausted, somehow, we increased our rate of fire. Little Cadet Lewis was not familiar with the firing of the artillery, but his role in our section was to get the ammo to the cannons. We could only fire as fast as the ammo was presented to us, and Cadet Lewis never failed us. He actually picked up his pace. It seemed the more we fired our cannons, the more the enemy started to find us as they began shelling in our direction. I felt like I was in hell. Smoke and fire all around. Shells were screaming over our heads; some burst all around us. I could not see their guns, but I sure felt them. My head was pounding, and it felt like my guts were bouncing around inside my body with every explosion. We were putting up a shit load of fire on those Yankees. I looked over at Corporal Henry, who was our gunner. He was resting beside the cannon, waiting for the next shell to be delivered. He looked at me with a big grin. He said, "Them Yankees sure started to shell us good. You look awfully scared, my friend."

"Henry," I said as calmly as I could, "shouldn't we move the heck out of here? They seemed to know where we are here."

"You don't understand, Pat. General Breckinridge wants us to show our position. He wants us to draw the fire of Sigel's cannons."

"Good God-man, why?" I began to think less of General Breckinridge at that moment.

Henry continued, "The general needs to know where Sigel's cannons are and how many. Now get back to the horses, as I think we will be moving out soon."

As I ran back to prepare the horses, I prayed he was right. At that moment, Minge rode up and said, "We are moving up the pike as the infantry advances. This is how we will do this. Berkeley's Battery will fire, then limber up and advance. Then we'll fire and do the same thing, and Chapman will repeat it while we're moving. We are going to leapfrog along this road. The general wants us to fire obliquely into the Union left without fear of hitting our own boys. Be ready. After the next volley, we'll move up!"

He didn't need to tell me twice as I was ready to move out of the enemy's cannon barrage. General Breckinridge's theory, to me, was not a tactic I had ever learned at the institute, but I liked the idea of constant movement. Once again, we stopped and unlimbered our guns, getting ready to fire. I looked over to my left, and through the darkness and rain, I could see the battle raging as our troops were charging up a hill. I swear the flag I could see was the VMI color flag. I called out to the cadet artillery, "Look out there to the left! I saw the VMI color flag charging up the hill!"

We all let out a yell. I know they could not hear us, but we began to put fire on the enemy more than ever, as we could see. They needed all the cover we could give them. It looked like they were running right into the depths of hell.

WHERE ARE MY FRIENDS AND FAMILY?

As we moved forward, the cannon and musket fire seemed to increase as the two great armies came closer to each other. We received orders from Breckenridge to maneuver our cannons up the pike and set up behind a low stone wall. Our artillery group of Chapman's battery, Berkeley's battery, and VMI battery arrived at the stone wall and unlimbered. Minge ordered us to load up the cannons with double loads of canisters. Minge had us aim the cannons to the right of the pike at some woods.

What are we waiting for? I thought to myself. *The battle is to our left.* Suddenly, I saw men in blue on horseback. It was a Yankee cavalry unit coming over a small crest. Minge yelled as loud as he could, "Fire!" Several of the men in blue never knew what hit them, as many men and horses were knocked over by our first blast. We fired continuously as the Yankees tried to retreat, but to my surprise, McLaughlin's cannons fired on them from the other direction. The Yankees had no idea where to run as we continued the cannon barrage from both sides. It was a site of mass confusion, as the horsemen had no idea where to retreat to. It was a brilliant ambush, and it routed the Yankee cavalry. According to Minge, we saved Breckinridge's right flank. I was very proud of the cadet's part, but the mass destruction of these men seemed for a moment like a meaningless slaughter. A slaughter of probably good men who had families, Moms, and Dads praying for the safe return of their sons from war. They would never see their loved ones again. Never give them a proper burial.

Suddenly, I remembered back at the institute, an old veteran who told me about war. I was at the institute sharing some spirits with my fellow cadets. We had been at it for some time, and we began to spout off of how glorious battle would be. We were ready to fight for our country. I remembered Willie Shaw saying, "Let's go find a Yankee and shoot him." That brought a laugh. An older man had been sitting next to us for a while. I noticed because he was well-dressed with a well-groomed beard. But when he got up to get himself another drink, he was missing a leg and an arm. What could have happened to him? I thought. He must be some kind of hero. While he was sitting there listening to our bravado, I could tell he was getting restless; maybe the proper word was agitated. Anyway, we had to get back to the institute. I had some spirit left to finish off, so I was sitting alone at the table. This man hobbled over and plopped down beside me.

I said, "Hello, sir, what can I do for you?"

He said, "Son, I lost my arm at the battle of Bull Run. I still had the spirit to fight. I lost my leg at the battle of Chancellorsville."

I was humbled by this man's bravery and was telling him so when he abruptly stopped me. Looking dead in my eyes, he said, "War is a waste of good people. It solves nothing. This war between the states will end someday, and we will have a country and a people who have been devastated beyond your comprehension. You are a young, strong boy, but you don't know war. It will change your mind and destroy your body. Look at me, I am not much good for anything. War is the devil's work, and no good comes from the devil. I hope you never have to experience it. I hope this war ends soon, or there will be nothing left to fight for. God bless you, son, and your fellow brave cadets."

With that, he hobbled off, out of the bar and down the street. *Boy, what a crazy old-timer*, I thought at the time.

That man was making good sense to me now, but I didn't have time to ponder while I was in the middle of the most hellacious battle I could ever imagine.

After the ambush, we turned our guns back up to the high ground and continued our cannon barrage. We could see from our position on the pike now the VMI flag for sure. It was just outside what looked like an orchard. We gave a loud VMI cheer for our fellow cadets who have now entered the battle they have long waited for. I'm sure they could not hear us through the noise of battle, but it felt good to cheer them on. But I could see they were marching into purgatory. I said a quiet prayer for my friends and then got back to laying down a constant fire to best protect them. We maintained our rate of fire on the enemy until the line had advanced too far to continue safely. Once again, we unlimbered and moved up the pike with our advancing soldiers.

After another hundred yards or so, we stopped and unlimbered. I could see the enemy up close for the first time. We are ordered to aim at the cannons at the top of the hill. I could see the flashes from the battery of Yankee cannons. I could see about six cannons all shooting toward our troops, who were bravely running right at them. I shouted to anyone who could hear me, "Let's blow the hell out of those guns!" I felt a pain in my leg like a wasp sting. Then I heard a loud thud, followed by an explosion. I looked around to my right and saw a cannon tipped over on its side, missing a wheel and a carriage upside down on fire. I knew I had to put that fire out quickly before it reached the bombs inside. I rushed over, took my jacket off, and tried to put the flames out. Cadet Lewis showed up beside me and started flinging handfuls of mud on the flames. Together, we kept the flames controlled until Corporal Henry and Cadet Seaborne arrived with buckets of water to put the flames out completely. I did not think to use the water bucket we use to clean out the barrels after firing the cannons. Nevertheless, we got a lot of pats on the back for quick action by Captain Minge. I was so intent on quelling the fire I didn't notice the dead bodies. Three men were killed, and one horse was down. Cadet Whitehead was wounded in his shoulder. I had to shoot the horse as it was wounded mortally and was a danger to the rest of the men. The three mangled bodies were left where they lay as we had to move again. My first sight of dead men and body parts splattered about. I swallowed the puke that came up in the back of my throat and went back to my cannon. I decided to get the cannon that killed my fellow Confederate soldiers so brutally. What a sight when we started to blast that Yankee battery. The Yankee fire slowed significantly. I could see over to the left our troops advancing up the hill at a good pace now. The cannons were not firing back at us. They seemed to be limbering up to move out. For the first time, I felt like we helped gain the edge in this godforsaken battle. My fellow cadets and I were firing our cannons at a high rate, almost as fast as the veterans. I could see the Yankees starting to retreat.

Quickly, an order yelled out, "Unlimber and advance as the Yanks are on the run."

I hitched up the horses and wagons and cannons. I hopped up on one of the wagons, grabbed the reins, and galloped up the pike. I could see the Yankees running back to the north now. Even over the battle noise, I could hear the rebels yell as they chased the enemy. We unlimbered our guns and fired in the general direction of the retreating Yanks. I felt excited. My heart was pounding as we continued to pour fire on the Yanks. I looked over to the top of Bushong Hill, and I could make out soldiers sitting on a cannon. It was in the spot we were firing on a moment ago. I could see a soldier sitting on a cannon waving a flag. It sure looked like the VMI flag. I hope and pray that it was VMI cadets who claimed that cannon. What a feat that would be if they captured an enemy cannon. I felt like maybe the cadet artillery also had a hand in capturing that cannon.

The enemy was retreating so fast we could hardly keep up with them. We continued chasing the enemy until we reached the hill. There we had a great view of the Yanks retreat and set our guns on them again. I have to say they did not turn tail and run. They stopped and held their ground for a short time before running again. But our continued shelling did not give any reason for them to come back south.

We had to stay alert as we were still receiving occasional fire from the Yanks. I looked over the hill and could see the Yankees were reforming their ranks and returning fire on our men. These Yanks were not running like the rest of the Union forces. We limbered up, and our unit galloped up the pike to fire on these Yanks. I was almost giddy as the atmosphere was lighthearted, and among us, there was good-natured banter. As we galloped down the pike, our young cadet Lewis, who I watched grow up on this journey, said to me with some disgust, "I wish those Yanks would just stop running and set up their guns. I would love a few more shots at the enemy."

We came up to about 200 yards from the slowly retreating Union forces, and they were setting up their artillery in our general location. Holy shit. This group of Yankees was slowing down our victory charge. Mr. Minge said to anyone listening, "This is the rear guard of Sigel's artillery." I did not care who they were as they had turned and were aiming their guns at us! I was happy that we would get another chance to fire our guns. We set to getting our guns in position to fire, and the mood was lighthearted. Captain Minge screamed, "They are firing. Take cover!" I dove behind a wagon.

WHERE ARE MY FRIENDS AND FAMILY?

Most other men lay flat on the ground. The mini balls hummed like honeybees as they flew by.

One of the older veterans climbed on a cannon and waved at the Yanks. He expressed his defiance by saying, "Y'all missed us again! You wasted a lot of ammo on that shot." I swore I heard a response from one of the Yanks, but I could not make out a word of it.

"Why don't we show those bastards how to shoot?" yelled Cadet Lewis. Everyone turned toward him with amazement.

A veteran looked over at him and said, "What did you say, young fella?"

Lewis looked him straight in the eye and repeated, "Let's shoot those bastards!"

Another veteran said, "Well, all right then. You men heard him."

We let out a blast toward the Yanks. The shells landed well short of their marks and stuck right in the mud, but it had the Yanks running for any type of cover they could find. We laughed and slapped each other on the back. For a moment, I forgot the last three hours of hell. The order was given to limber up and advance toward the retreating enemy. The smoke got so dense I could not see much of anything, but we continued to push down the pike. I figured we must have advanced about three miles while chasing the Union Army. We stopped at a small grove of trees on the right side of the pike road. We looked up the road Sigel had set up the cannons he had left on the ridge and were shelling our men who were chasing the fleeing Yanks.

Here, we unlimbered our guns and set up to return fire on the ridge. I knew that cannon fire was killing our pursuing rebel heroes. The cadets, along with McLaughlin's artillery, began shelling the ridge. I heard Captain Minge say in a whisper, "Those fellas right now are the only ones that seem to have any fight left in 'em. Look at all those others running away. We will never catch them."

Well, we tried to catch the Yanks. Under Mr. Berkeley's command, the artillery charged down the hard road like a cavalry unit, and I was forced to keep up or be run over by the veteran's wagons. Our wagons (cadets) had just been reloaded up with munitions and were rolling very loosely. All I heard was Mr. Minge yelling, "We need to get to the crest of Rude's hill."

We were firing on Sigel's remaining army just as they were crossing the bridge. It was getting dark, and we could not see the enemy well. I hoped some shells found their mark. We continued to fire until General Breckinridge rode up to our battery. We all stopped what we were doing and stared at our commander. General Breckinridge stared back at us for a few seconds, looking into every cadet's eyes. He said, "Young men, I have to thank you for the result of today's actions. I am proud of you. More than I can express. You have done more than your share for the day, and I can ask you to do no more. You may fall out and rest here. The remainder of the army can take care of Mr. Sigel."

The general rode off in all his glory. I and the rest of the cadets literally fell to the ground. It was like my body went limp. I was working and fighting on pure fear mixed with excitement, and my body just quit. I heard Mr. Breckinridge shout back at us as he rode off, "Well done, Virginians! Well done!"

What a feeling. I could see down below a flicker of red light. It grew in size until it was very bright. I asked Captain Minge what it was. With a happy look on his face, he said, "That is the bridge that Sigel needs to cross, and we have just burned his only escape from us. We have him trapped. This victory will soon be complete."

The cadets were ordered to set camp in the tree grove, which was fine with me as it was the driest place I'd seen in four days. The camp was full of vigor as everyone swapped stories of heroic deeds. I'm sure most were exaggerated, as some of mine were just a little. The veterans had a different opinion of us now, and they treated us as equals. Some of the vets used the term heroic when talking about our part in the battle. I was proud to be a VMI cadet and to be alive to enjoy the praise, but I am going to take a long nap. The sounds of war were far from us now and winding down. I had found a nice dry spot under the trees.

The next day after the battle, it was still foggy and dreary, but the rain had stopped. Hallelujah! Mr. Minge had orders for us to join the rest of the cadets at a campsite just outside of town. The townspeople were out of their houses, welcoming us as we marched proudly to the camp. Once there, the war vets who insulted and

WHERE ARE MY FRIENDS AND FAMILY?

embarrassed us before now showered us with honor. The glory of battle was all that I thought it would be.

In camp, I didn't see many cadets. I asked the nearest soldier, "Where are the cadets?"

He turned to me and said, "Your friends are now learning the hell of war. They are out looking for their wounded and dead."

"O dear God, I must go out and find my fellow cadets." George and Henry, along with Lewis and I, left camp to search for our friends, and I was praying all were safe even though I knew from what I saw on the battlefield many must be hurt. A bad feeling had come over me, and I immediately thought back about my conversation with Cadet Stanard by the campfire. I wondered whether his premonition had come true. I pray it did not.

We went house to house in search of our wounded friends. Finally, we entered a home that had many wounded. Our doctors, Madison and Ross, were there helping the wounded. The house was full of wounded soldiers from both sides, and the smell of death was horrific. The wood floors were red stained.

Lewis asked under his breath, "Is that blood?" His eyes were big and filled with tears. I wiped my eyes as the groans and cries were overbearing, and I had to run out. Standing just outside was Cadet Atwill.

"Where the hell are you going, Pat?"

"Sam, I am glad to see you. Your leg is bleeding?"

"I will have a battle scar to show my kids someday," he said proudly.

"You shouldn't be outside. You should be in a hospital."

"Naw. I'm a lucky one. Don't worry for me," Sam said as bravely as he could.

I could tell his leg was hurting. "Sam, what do you know about our friends?" I asked, not really sure I wanted to know.

He took a long, deep breath and, with a slightly choked-up voice, said, "Five of our brave friends are dead. A ceremony will be held at the St. Matthew's Church this afternoon."

"Who were they?"

"Cadets Cabell, Mcdowell, Crocket, and Jones. All these cadets were friends, Pat. The cadet corps had about thirty-seven wounded," Sam went on to say. He asked me, "How did the artillery do?"

I was very proud to say, "We pounded the hell out of them and chased the Yanks for miles. We saw the bridge was burning, so them Yanks were trapped like rats."

Atwill smiled at my bravado but said, "Unfortunately, our forces could not get to the bridge in time, and the Yanks were able to cross over and burn the bridge behind them. But the day was ours, and we fought as well or better than any soldier on the field. Any cadets wounded in artillery. Scraps and bruises, mostly except for Mr. Whitehead. He got hit in the shoulder. I'm not sure how he is yet. How did you do, Pat? I notice some redness on your right leg."

I suddenly remembered the sting I felt. I reached down to feel the red spot, and sure enough, I had been wounded.

"Maybe you should get checked by a surgeon?"

I couldn't tell if Sam was being an asshole about my teeny wound or seriously concerned. When he couldn't conceal his laughter, I knew he was being an asshole.

"I'll be just fine, Sam. I appreciate your concern. But seriously, we need to check on our friends."

"I agree, but I think I will rest right here for a while," Sam said as he managed to find a nice, comfortable stump to sit on.

In my mind, I was very worried about Sam's leg wound, but he said he was okay, and I needed to find more of my friends.

Mr. Lewis and I walked to the battlefield to see for ourselves the end result of the battle. We thought maybe we could help find anyone who was still alive and maybe collect some trophies from our victory, but once we got to the field, well, the death smell was too pungent. The destruction everywhere was overwhelming, and I didn't need any trophies to remind me of this battle. Lewis and I went back to camp. Sam was still sitting on that stump, looking at me like he was hurting pretty bad. Before I could tell him to go get some medical attention for his leg, he said, "Jack Stanard met his fate. He was wounded and died a few hours ago." Sam continued, "He was told to guard the supply wagons away from the battle, but you know

Jack, he followed his friends into battle. If he had followed orders, he would be alive and probably boasting that the cadets would have captured two cannons instead of only one if he had been with them."

I thought, *Oh my god. He actually saw his death, and it came true.* It seemed to me that fate is not definite, as it gave Jack a choice to avoid the battle. Jack chose to go with fate and with his friends. He would be missed.

The residents of New Market were very appreciative of our efforts in the battle and treated us like heroes. They welcomed us into their homes and offered food and drink until we could hold no more. Even the older veterans slapped us on the back and shook our hands. I believe we finally got their respect. Wet and exhausted, we had gained the respect and admiration of everyone in town. We bore our hardships without complaint. But then it occurred to me, of course, we did. We are VMI cadets.

I did have some sympathy for the Union wounded. The townspeople refused to bring the Yankee wounded into their houses. They had a hate for the Yankees that was deep and cold, and they would just as well let the wounded die and lie out in the field. No Union soldiers were buried in the town cemetery. Most were buried where they fell in shallow graves. Whoever wins this war (or outlasts the other) will have a hard time putting everyone back into one happy country. My fear is it may not be possible.

The remains of our friends who died were put into handmade caskets and taken to St. Matthew's Cemetery. A brief ceremony was offered, and the five caskets were gently lowered into the ground. I sobbed like a baby. I wasn't alone, as not a single cadet had a dry eye. We all needed a good cry as the past five days had been the highest point in our young lives and the lowest point in our lives. We have become veterans of war, and it has changed us. I don't know how, but I feel I have been through something that has given me a new perspective on people and how I should conduct myself from now on. I know I love my fellow cadets like I never have. I guess I want to be a better man. I have seen the beast in me, and I don't want to see that part of me again. These thoughts are scaring me as they are way too deep. I want to go home now.

General Breckinridge released us to go back to school, but as I heard it, General Imboden argued the cadets needed to go to Richmond to help guard the city, and this would allow badly needed veterans to go to the front with General Lee and destroy Mr. Grant. I guess General Imboden's argument was accepted as we marched out of New Market and headed to Harrisonburg. We arrived in Harrisonburg on May 20, with no time to linger as we marched to and arrived in Staunton on May 21. The marching was not so bad as every place or town we marched through or by had heard of our bravery at New Market, and the people came out, waved, and cheered. They offered their houses for us to rest in, but, of course, we couldn't accept that, but we did get plenty of cakes and food to eat. Even marching ten to fifteen miles a day, I think I gained five pounds. But the most amazing experience was the young ladies. Before the battle, the girls treated us like boys. "Look how cute they look in their uniforms" was a common remark. But now they treated us as men. Veterans, warriors of the South. I might be exaggerating a bit, but the ladies looked at us differently after the battle, and that was great! In Staunton, the town threw us a party. Plenty of nice young ladies, and they all wanted to dance with a cadet. I had my share of dances, but my heart belonged to a girl back in Currituck County, and I was terribly, terribly true to her, and that is all I have to say about that.

We went by railroad to Richmond and arrived there on May 23. We set up camp at Camp Lee. The cadets were reviewed and addressed by government dignitaries. It was very exciting to see our government leaders praise us for our bravery, but boy, can they talk for hours about nothing. It got old quickly. One much-needed gift was awarded to us by the secretary of war. Brand-new uniforms. New uniforms were about the best gift we received. Believe me, people could spell the cadets of VMI a mile away coming to their town. We washed our old uniforms, but the smell of war would not wash out. The next best part of being a hero was the parties. Several of my friends were having quite a time with the young ladies. Not me though, as you can ask anybody. But you can't trust what they might say, so I would just believe me. It was nice to be called heroes everywhere we went. But soon reality set in, and we were sent to help build defensive trenches around Richmond. Hard, dirty work in the hot sun, but we dug some of the best-looking defensive lines around Richmond. Bringing in the cadets allowed the exit of many soldiers to go and join Lee at the war's front lines. Once again, we were placed in a secondary position in case we were needed. To tell the truth, I was okay with that.

On May 28, we were transferred to Carter's Farm and assigned to duty under General GWC Lee, commanding the local defense troops. Once again, we prepared defensive positions at the intermediate line, midway between Brook and Meadow Bridge roads, and continued in this camp until June 6. We received orders to return to Lexington. We finally returned to our institute on the ninth. What a very trying journey to get back home. The first half of our journey was exciting as we were the toast of town everywhere we went. In Richmond, we were back in the trenches. Digging them, not fighting them.

The first person at the institute to greet me was Willie Shaw, my best friend. He wanted to be with us in battle so badly, but he was in the infirmary, sick as a dog.

"Pat, how was it? Did you kill any Yanks? I heard you captured a cannon."

"Hold on there, Willie. I was in the artillery, and we took a lot of shots at the Yanks, so I assumed we got some of them. But it was the infantry that captured a cannon." I continued on by saying, "Willie, it was glorious in the victory, but some of our boys were killed and many wounded."

"Yes, I know," Willie said. "I heard that five cadets were killed, and forty-eight were wounded. I wish I could have been there with you all."

"I know, but let's get something to drink, and I will tell you all about it."

I couldn't believe it. The very next day, we got word that the Union forces were approaching Lexington. On June 11, we could hear artillery and sharpshooter fire in the hills north of town. We told Commander Smith we were ready to fight, but he told us we were to stand down as other soldiers were fighting this battle. Well, apparently, that Confederate force withdrew back and allowed General Hunter's forces to move closer to Lexington. I had just gotten back to my old room (45). Jule, Robert, and I spent the time in our room talking about our battle experiences. That left Willie out of the conversation because he was in the infirmary with a high temperature and was not allowed to go with us when we got the call to go to New Market. He was a very good listener, but we could tell his disappointment. Boy, there was some lying going on as each story got a little bit more unbelievable as the night went on. We all said a prayer for our roomie, Atwill, as he is recovering well in the infirmary. I was surprised to find a letter from home on my desk. It was dated May 16. It was from my pa. The funny part about this letter is it was written before Pa knew I was in the Battle of New Market on May 15. I sent him a letter about my participation in the battle soon after, but he did not get it for weeks after the battle. All the guys wanted to have it read out loud, so I read Pa's letter out loud.

The actual letter was on May 16, 1864.

> My Dear Son,
>
> I embrace the opportunity this morning, as Mr. Forbs is just going out, to write you a few lines to let you know we have had the pleasure of receiving yours of the 26th of April, that we were all well and made still more happy on hearing glorious news from Virginia. The New York Herald admits that Grant has been terribly whipped and driven back with loss of only 41,000, including 7 Major Generals and some 15 brigadiers. We have rumors that the Yanks have also been badly worsted near Petersburg and driven back with considerable loss. Also various other rumors of the capture of the "beast". Which if true you have no doubt heard of this, as you learn the truth much earlier than we can. Should these things be true, this fanatical war must be drawing rap-

idly to a close. May God speed the happy day. I think there could scarcely be a doubt of the truth of Grant's disaster. I did not see the statement myself, but Mr. Hilliard Baxter told me he had read it in last Thursday's Herald and you maybe sure his loss is much greater than the Herald would admit.

The Yanks have been making frequent raids among us for the last three weeks, one a week at least. Saturday night they carried off one of my mules, but I was fortunate enough to recover him on Sunday. I am glad to learn you were pleased with your things. The boots and gloves I expected would be full large, but it was the best I could do, and your clothes, how do they suit you? It was nearest the color that could be got.

We have felt a great deal of anxiety about you of late, fearing that the yankees would get so near you would have to take the field again, but if Grant is driven back we should feel much easier on that account. I forgot to say our joy at the good news was somewhat allayed by a report that the brave and noble Gen. Longstreet was badly wounded, Picket and Jenkins and some others killed. I trust the reports may not be true, but should it be true, God will raise up others to fill their places. He will not suffer our enemies to succeed in this unjust, cruel and unholy war.

I said we are all well. Jodie has slight chills and fevers, caused perhaps by the days of the measles; he says he wants to see bro mighty bad. He has been keeping you some apples but has been compelled to eat them to keep them from rotting. The children all sent their love. Mr. Low and family request me to send their respects.

Mrs. Shaw and family are well. Give my respect to Willie, Jule and all your friends. Write often.

May a kind providence continue to watch over you and protect you, my dear son.

Your father J.B.M.

We all giggled as our families had no idea we just fought in a major battle. "Except you, Willie, of course, you were sick," I said jokingly. The look in Willie's eyes told me right away I had made a terrible joke. "I'm sorry, Willie, that was a terrible joke. I'm sorry."

"When I get my chance, I will make up for missing out at New Market."

"I know you will, Willie, as every cadet here knows you as one of the best cadets here."

Jule seconded that opinion.

"Okay, then I forgive you, Pat. But I don't ever want to hear you talk like that again, even in joking."

"On my ma's head, I will never joke about that again. Whew, I crossed the line that time. Once again, Willie," I said, "I am sorry."

We marched out of VMI on June 11, and within hours, the Union Army marched into the grounds of VMI. We should have stayed and defended our school. We had orders to leave, and as a soldier, you followed orders. But if we had known they were going to burn our school, maybe those orders would have been different. I would have liked to think so. All cadets gathered their belongings or as much as they could carry. We marched to the mouth of the North Anna River, where we set up camp. Four days of guard duty near Balcony Falls. No Yankees showed up, as we thought they were coming that way. Eventually, we were ordered to report to Lynchburg. We took a position on the north side of the river for a week or so, then we were ordered back to Lexington. I have never walked so many miles as I did last month. I saw no action but dug a lot of holes, or some might call defensive positions. As we marched in, the site of our school being burnt down was disgusting. Those damn Yankees had no right to burn our institution, our home. We knew we should have stayed and met the enemy on our ground. I am sure it was done for revenge since we kicked them in the nuts at New Market. Fortunately, the Yanks decided not to burn Washington College, so we set up temporary quarters in those buildings.

I had enough of war, and now my school was destroyed. I was exhausted by marching, and while sitting in my room at Washington College, I decided it was time to go home. To my surprise and happiness, Superintendent Smith on June 27 called us to assemble. He told us how well we performed and that he was proud of us. That was very nice, but the best news was he furloughed all cadets. He said we should report back to the almshouse in Richmond in late September. At that time, all academia would start again. Once Mr. Smith said, "Dismissed," every cadet jumped with relief as most of us thought we would be called back out to Richmond to dig more defensive works and guard duty and march more. I remember talking with an old veteran one time. I asked him about the glory of battle. I was new at the institution. He told me, "Son, all war is marching around the country looking for a fight and very often not finding one. More soldiers died of disease, accidents, and bad food than in battle. I hope you find your glory one day, but I haven't." I thought at the time he was delusional, or maybe he was a Yankee veteran. I now think he nailed it. War is a terrible way to solve problems. Anyway, I am going home. Now I have to figure out a way to get past the Union forces to see my family. I don't think the Yankees consider the VMI cadets as schoolboys anymore.

I rounded up Willie Shaw and Julian Wood and said, "Boys, let's go home." We all hugged and laughed. We were going home. But to what, as none of us knew what was left of our homes, families, and friends. We got our furloughs as we needed them to show the Yankees that we were students only and we were going home from school. I hoped that was enough to get us through the Yankee checkpoints.

Willie said, "Do you think because we were in a battle, they will consider us enemy soldiers and take us to prison?"

"I don't know, but I'm going home anyway," I said with more confidence than I felt. "Let's get packed up."

We all got together to plan our trip home to Currituck County, North Carolina. I started the conversation by suggesting a train route home. "I think the train route is best."

"I don't know," said Willie. "The Yankees would be all over the railways and nervous about Confederate spies looking to sabotage the rails."

"Yeah," said Jule, "those Yanks might be more apt to hold us up."

"Good points were made, but I checked out a route I think would be mostly safe. We will get through the Yankee checkpoint at Lexington as they know us (VMI students), and they just burned our school down. I think they will let us pass. Then we go to Charlottesville, which is still Confederate, on to Richmond, and to Norfolk. In Norfolk, we might have problems, but the Yanks have this town under control, and I don't think they will worry about three students returning home from school. The last leg is to Elizabeth City. We notify our people to meet us there, and by horse and carriage, we get home."

"Not bad, Pat, but still risky. Maybe we should just stay here for a while where we know it is safe."

"Safe for how long? I am sorry to say that the Yankees have taken Lexington and are on the move. We stopped them in New Market, but we just bloodied their noses. They will be coming to Staunton and to Richmond soon. We will be cut off completely by rail then. No, we can't wait. We must go now."

"You are right, Pat," Willie said. "We must move out now."

I knew Willie was with me as he always liked an adventure, and if he got a chance, he would love to take a few Yankees out. He was still hurting over the fact he could not go with us to New Market to get some revenge on the Yankees for killing his father. He was ill in the infirmary with a high fever that made him delirious the day we marched out to New Market.

"Okay then, here is our route back home," I said. "We take the train out of Lexington. This will be the most dangerous, I think, as the Yanks will be most distrustful of us cadets. We may have to sign a paper that we will be neutral toward the war. I know that will be dishonest, boys, but we will have to sign. From Lexington, we go to

WHERE ARE MY FRIENDS AND FAMILY?

Charlottesville. That town is still free of Yankees, and there will be no problem going to Richmond and Norfolk. Here, we will need to pass by a serious Yankee checkpoint, but with our school papers and a paper from the Lexington Yankee checkpoint, we should be good to go on to Elizabeth City, where our folks or friends can get us home to Currituck by horse and wagon. The Yankees know of my father as to be a neutral farmer, and I am sure they will allow us, even though we kicked their Yankee asses at New Market, to pass through to get home. Tomorrow we go. Sleep well, boys, for tomorrow night, we could be home snuggled in our beds or off to a Yankee military prison."

"Shit, Pat, that was a perfect thought for us to sleep on," Willie said. "That's why I will be carrying my pistol."

"You can't do that, Willie. They will take your gun and consider you a Confederate soldier, and all of us will be in deep shit."

"I was just joshing, Pat. You need to relax."

"Great, Willie, I just don't know when you are joshing or dead serious." I'm still not sure what Willie might do. I thought about that all night.

We all gathered at the train depot at sunrise. Nothing but blue coats around, and they were watching us closely. The Yankee in the ticket booth asked me if I was a cadet from the military school up on the hill. My small breakfast dashed back up in my mouth. "Yes, sir," I said. "We, three cadets, are heading home as the cadets have been furloughed from school."

"You don't say. I think maybe I should arrest you three right now. Send you to prison." He smiled, or he could have if he had any teeth.

Three or four soldiers came over with bayonets pointing at our chest and asked him, "Are these boys giving you shit, Sergeant?"

"Yea," the sergeant said. "Why don't you march their little rebel asses to the guardhouse. I will decide on what to do with them over the next few weeks."

I grabbed Willie's arm as I felt him move toward the soldiers. I repeated to the sergeant that we were students and not Confederate soldiers. I said this loudly, hoping someone would hear and help us.

I heard a loud and strong voice say, "Sergeant!" The sergeant snapped to attention. "Stop scaring these lads to death. As you know, by order of General Hunter, all VMI cadets will be free to return home." The old sarge was quick to apologize for his behavior and asked us very politely, "Do you wish to buy a train ticket?"

Very half-hearted apology, in my opinion, I thought, but what a relief. The sarge gave each of us tickets all the way through to Elizabeth City with passports to use at Yankee checkpoints. It looks like we just might make it home. The train was very comfy, and at each depot we stopped at, there was water and cookies available for the passengers. Everything was going nicely until we stopped at the Norfolk depot. A group of Yankee soldiers who were coming on board looked at us like we just stole something.

Willie said, "You have a problem, fellas?" Up till now, Willie had been very understanding that we were in hostile territory, and he had been very accommodating to the looks and occasional jabs at us by other passengers. Willie stood up tall and, without saying a word, threw a majestic haymaker against the jaw of the biggest soldier. Down that soldier went. *Oh my lord*, I thought. I would just act like I didn't know him and let the soldiers take him away. But the VMI spirit of "leave no man behind" kicked in. Jule was the first to jump up with fists ready, and then I jumped up in my fighting stance. My heart was pumping 'cause nothing good would come of this. The soldiers were shell-shocked. One of the soldiers looked at Willie and said, "Why did you do that? I think you broke his jaw."

Willie shot back, "Do you want the same?"

"I sure don't, and neither do my friends," said the Yank. He looked at his friend on the floor and said, "We don't want any trouble. We just want to get home to our families. We've had enough fighting and killing to last a lifetime."

With that thought, we all agreed to shake hands and peacefully enjoy our ride home. We even joined in a drink or two and toasted to the end of the war. Nobody even thought about suggesting who the victor may be.

As the six of us commiserated about our war, I noticed one of our new friends was very quiet and aloof. I went over to him and sat down beside him. His name was Jackson Smith. I asked him what was on his mind as he was in his own world it seemed. Jackson looked me dead in my eyes and said, "You are a VMI cadet, aren't you?"

I was very proud to say I was.

He said, "I was at the Battle of New Market." He continued, "Lost a lot of good friends there. I was with Maj. General Julius Stahel's cavalry. We charged the rebs, who had retreated to a tree line. We had them on the run and were going to finish them off. Out of nowhere, a barrage of cannon fire erupted. My best friend was hit in the face. His brains sprayed out on me. That same shell continued on to take the shoulder off the man behind him, killing him, and went through the chest of the man behind him." The Yank took a deep breath. "I remember thinking, where did that shell come from? Then all hell broke loose, as cannon fire and musket fire came forth from the right side of us. I could see the batteries up on a hill to the right of us. Then the rebs from the tree line regrouped and began an intense rate of fire right in front of us. It was a massacre of epic proportions. We had nowhere to go except to retreat, and we could not regroup as we were decimated. The battlefield was covered with dead cavalrymen and horses. We were effectively taken out of the battle. The battle was decided then. The damn rebels took our left flank and attacked with gusto through it. I can't sleep at night as the nightmares are unbearable. Every night, I wake up in a sweat. The army is sending me down to Elizabeth City, where I can rest and do paper shoveling."

Oh my good lord, I was there firing my cannon at him. I never thought I would meet a man that I was trying to kill. He described in detail the destruction we did that day. It was hard to hear even though our hatred of Yankees was real, and we thought, at the time, they deserved what we gave them. I felt sympathy for this man. Everyone will be scarred for life from this war. Can we really repair the country after so much death and destruction? Can Yankee and Confederate soldiers forgive each other? One day, you are trying to kill each other, and a day later, we have to live together in harmony. I believe that if our country survives, it may take generations for the hatred to be forgotten. Can a whole group of people who have been considered less than human and kept ignorant blend into the White man's society? I don't know. Too serious for me. I slipped back over to my friends and enjoyed the rest of the trip to Elizabeth City.

Elizabeth City was full of people. Unfortunately, most were wearing Union uniforms. But I was glad that the city was still intact and people were doing their business. The war seemed far away from here, and that felt good. As I looked around, I saw my pa and ma coming down the road. They were waving and calling my name. That moment was the happiest I've been in my life.

Needless to say, the reunion with my family was wonderful. My brother Frank was eighteen years old now and had been practicing medicine with Dr. Colwell. Jodie, my little brother, was proud to have for me several apples that he had been saving for me. Those apples looked terrible, as he had been saving them apparently for quite a while, but I received them with a smile. My sisters, Lydia, who was twelve years old, and Ida, who was nine years old, were growing up to be very lovely ladies, but I was worried about Lydia as she couldn't seem to shake the fevers at night. It seemed that this type of illness had been common in the area. Pa's farm was in bad shape.

There were no Negro workers or White workers to be had as the Yankees had freed all the Black slaves, and all the White men had gone to fight on their chosen side. Only old people were left to work the farms.

"Dad, they want me back at school in late September, so we need to get to work on this farm."

I had never worked so hard these two months in my life. Even digging ditches at Richmond was not this tiring. Willie and Jule came over when they could to help out. The trouble with that was we always went down to the local watering hole to cool down with a few cold beers and occasional local moonshine after the sun went down. This troubled my pa as he thought Willie was a bad influence on me, but he loved Willie like a son and respected his father, Colonel Shaw. He was right about Willie; he could be belligerent and hardheaded, but I always wanted him on my side. Jules and I thought of Willie as our bodyguard. People in the area respected him, let's say, for his ability to defend himself. Oftentimes in the bar, discussions about the war could get heated, and more than once, Willie would settle down any discussions that got too heated. His father, Colonel Shaw, was a hero to most of the locals. Being home was not all work as I courted my girl, Mary Sara Deford. I thought she was the one, but I couldn't make a commitment until this war was done. But I thought she knew how I felt and that we had a future. At least, I hoped she did.

My best friend, Frank, came by today. I asked him, "Where did you go, Frank? Pa really needs help at the farm."

"I know, Master Pat," he said, "but when the Yankees freed all the slaves, I had to make a choice. I love your pa and ma, but freedom was given to me, and I had a chance to begin a free life on Roanoke Island. I was given an acre of land to live on and farm. The Yankees promised to build schools and churches and a community just for the Negroes. I also met an angel and married her."

"Frank," I said, "you've been a busy man since I've been gone. I am so happy for you. Your dream is coming true, and I am glad I got to see it happen. I only worry that so many Negroes may not be so fortunate."

"Pat, I'm no fool. I know that freedom will be hard, but the Negro people will need some help from the Whites. They have kept us down for so long that it will take a generation for us to catch up in education, and I pray a time will come when we can be considered American. That a Negro man and a White man can be thought of as just Americans, and slavery can be forgotten."

"I pray for that too, Frank. But I am afraid of the future. The hatred from this war has torn us apart. This country may never heal. It might take several generations for the country to come together."

"I hope you are wrong, Pat, but listen, I am here now, and what can I do to help you today?"

"Well, let's look around. I am sure we can find something. It's awfully good to see you again, Frank. I can already see several jobs we can do together. Let's get to it, brother—" Frank smiled—"like old times. I think after we get this work done, the ole fishing hole may be calling us," I said with a smile. "I have waited a long time to get back to that fishing hole."

My Pp helped out people whose lives had been destroyed by the war. He formed a network of farmers who were able to reap a decent crop. All the farmers agreed that Pa would be the best (most honest) man to distribute the food to the people who needed it. Sometimes, when someone would donate a cow or pig, Pa would invite all the locals for a barbecue. People would bring what they could, such as pies or fruits and vegetables. These gatherings of the community kept everybody's spirits up, and people got to know their neighbors better. I would see Pa go into the house with different men. I wondered what he was talking to them about, so I asked him.

"Pa, I notice you go into the house and talk to these men. What is going on?"

"Well, son, I have some knowledge about getting crops to market through the Yankee lines without them Yanks stealing it. Last year, a General Nagler sent a letter to the citizens of Currituck County. It said that if no future hostile act would be committed, the citizens would be allowed to sell their goods in Norfolk. This was a blessing as we were restricted from passing persons between Currituck and North River landing unless we had a pass from the provost marshal. This prevented us from trading freely, and Norfolk was the place to do business."

"So what happened next? Did you accept his conditions?"

"How could we? The leaders of the community got together and decided to respond with a letter. You know most of the people involved, such as Thomas Sanderson, John Barnard, EF Baxter, BM Baxter, and a few others. We wrote back, 'We would be delighted to reestablish trade in Norfolk,' but with this candid statement of facts, hoping and believing that with a knowledge of them will no longer hold us responsible for what we cannot possibly control."

"I bet that irked them a bit?"

"Well, about a month later, a letter from General Butler from up in Elizabeth City came to us. Our group met with him in person last year. I reported to him our difficulties in making a living without the ability to trade our goods in Norfolk. I noted to him that maybe allowing the people to ease their suffering from the war would reduce the civil unrest in Currituck."

WHERE ARE MY FRIENDS AND FAMILY?

"What did the letter say, Pa?"

"General Butler allowed a few of us to trade freely and send our goods through to Norfork with the promise we, the leaders of the county, would do our best to stop the attacks on Yankee soldiers. So you see, I was granted a pass to Norfolk. I can go through the Yankee checkpoints easily with my pass. I formed a group of businesses that trade in Norfolk through me. The people I am talking with are the businessmen I help get their goods to Norfork. I take care of the financial end for them."

"That's a great idea, Pa. I am so proud of you."

"Thank you, son. I am quite proud of you also. Let's go back to the picnic, son. There's a pie there with my name on it."

Mr. Sawyer and his wife had been with Pa on the farm for as long as I could remember. Today, they informed Pa they were moving out. I had been home for about two months, and with Pa, Frank, me, and Mr. Sawyer, we did well working the farm. But now I was getting ready to go back to school in Richmond, and with Mr. Sawyer leaving soon, I was concerned that Pa couldn't do it by himself. Of course, Pa said he could find help and not worry about him. "Mr. Lowe and his boys will help me when needed. You just stay out of the war the best you can."

I didn't see how I could avoid the war. I swear, after the New Market battle, I was not in a hurry to experience battle again.

I was concerned for my sister Lydia. She had been dealing with measles. My youngest brother had the measles first and had been feeling better, but Lydia was not doing well. The doctor had done all he could and recommended to keep her comfortable. She had to beat this on her own. There was no medicine that could do it. She was a fighter.

Lydia passed away this morning, August 12, 1864. She was twelve years old. I was with the rest of the family in her room when she died. My pa had seen many of his children die. Six children of his eleven so far, but he continued doing what he had to do to take care of his family. I didn't know how he managed it with a war happening all around him. My respect for my father and mother grew as they tackled every tragedy and heartbreak with powerful resourcefulness that only their faith in God could give them. God bless them, for I know God has blessed me by giving me parents like them.

It was the end of October, and it was time to head back to school. I believe the cadets would be situated at the almshouse in Richmond. The war was tilting toward the Yankees, and Richmond was the city we must hold, or all would be lost.

I saw Willie and Jule coming up the lane. It was time for me to go back to school.

"Hey, fellow cadets, ready for the academy?" I said with a huge grin.

"I doubt we would stay in school for six months as the damn Yankees will be in Richmond soon," a hostile Willie commented.

Jule looked at him with surprise and said, "Then, Willie, why are you even going back?"

Looking a little timid, he said, "Ma is making me go. She said she made a promise to my dad that I would graduate college before I go fight in the great war."

I said, "Good lord, I hope the war is over before then!"

Willie and Jule laughed at that. "Ma made me a big lunch, enough for the other boys if they were hungry."

The trip to Richmond was long. A lot of Yankee checkpoints to get through. We arrived safely and reported to the almshouse. It was great to see our cadet friends again and catch up. The worst news I heard was that Sam Atwill died from his wounds on July 20. He died from lockjaw caused by his wound at New Market. He was doing great when I saw him last.

I could not believe it. Cadet Brockenbrough came over to me. "Pat, I'll tell you what happened. Sam decided to go down to Harrisonburg on a visit, and he was feeling good. He apparently took a cold bath. He returned the next day to Lexington feeling unwell. He was taken with a lockjaw. Notwithstanding, it was feared, and everything was done to prevent it. Nothing availed. After three days of agony and suffering, he died. I will tell you, Pat, in his moments of clarity, he expressed a perfect knowledge of his situation and seemed to feel at peace. I heard his father did not learn of his death until August. Sam was buried at the school in a public cemetery where the gallant youth who fell at the sanguinary Battle of New Market will be laid to rest."

"How do you know all this, Robert?"

"I was with him in Lexington when he died."

We'd been at the almshouse for about a week when news came for the VMI corps to move out. We were going to Fort Lee to dig entrenchments and drill the new recruits. One thing VMI cadets do well is drill. It was a hot and dirty job digging in the dirt, but the cadets dug the best entrenchments we could because we understood that we could be in those holes in the coming battle for Richmond.

As we sat around a campfire, Willie wondered out loud, "What was the true number of cadets killed in action?"

Jule said that he heard that ten cadets died in battle and about fifty were wounded.

"That's about what I heard too," added Willie.

"We showed them we would fight, didn't we, boys?" I said loudly as the group all cheered. But everybody felt the pain of a friend who died or was maimed for life. War is horrible, and everyone who fought knew they paid a price, as the sights and sounds of battle will never be forgotten. The only good thing about being here in Richmond is we don't have any academic studies to worry about. Pardon my English.

We got orders on the twenty-seventh of October to head over to Poe's Farm as infantry support for a nearby battery. Digging entrenchments and defensive positions and drilling every day. It was getting colder, and the cadets did not have adequate winter clothing. In December, we left Poe's Farm to return to the almshouse in Richmond. It was cold, and some of the boys were granted a ten-day furlough to procure clothing and supplies. Then something terrible happened. Academics began again by the end of December. We continued to dig and reinforce the defensive positions around Richmond and had our studies to boot. Most of us did not see the sense in this as the Yankees were coming, and book learning was not going to stop them. I am glad to say that I believe the Yankees prefer to starve us out rather than fight. Devious devils, as this strategy is working well. I got a letter from my pa today. It was dated October 31, 1864.

How did this letter find me here? I held on to it until my watch was over and found my boys Willie and Jule. We were sitting around a big warm campfire when I said, "Boys, I received a letter from home today."

"What," said Willie, "how did they find you?"

"I don't know how, but what a blessing to hear from home."

"Read it out loud, Pat," said Jule. "I haven't gotten a letter for months."

"Me either," said Willie. "How did you get a letter delivered in your trench, Pat?"

Amazing postal service, I thought. The actual letter was dated October 31, 1864.

> My Dear Son,
>
> After so long a time I find an opportunity of sending you a few lines from home, as I know you are very anxious to hear from us all. Your note from Riddick's Ferry was received, though not until we heard from you through your friend from Kitty Hawk and who also delivered me a package of smoking tobacco, which was very acceptable. And for which accept my thanks. We have had a good long respite from the Rangers, not having been troubled with any since you left. They have passed on the Indian Town Road once since, but not coming up our road. There is no news at all. Everything seems to be at a stand. We are still having the most beautiful weather. It is so dry we can scarcely get water to use. I have never seen so dry a season. Mr. Lowe and myself have just finished making syrup. We have made about 70 gals., enough to serve us the next year plentifully. I am again without any help at all. Mr. Sawyer and his wife left the week you went

WHERE ARE MY FRIENDS AND FAMILY?

away. I do not know how I shall manage to house my crop as there are no laborers to be had.

A few days after you left I saw the order postponing the commencement of your school until the tenth of Novr., and ordering the Cadets to report for temporary duty at Camp Lee. I suppose you are still there, though according to the order will soon leave for school. I shall therefore leave the direction of my letter to the friend who will take it out after he can ascertain your whereabouts.

We are all in as good health as usual. I am still very much troubled with rheumatism in my arm, which bothers me very much. You must write me every opportunity, tell me how you are getting on and how you have disposed of your money, and do not forget, nor neglect, your duties to your heavenly Father; let not your young and gay companions lead you astray, nor tempt you to neglect your religious duties and may our heavenly Father keep you as in the hollow of his hand, shield and protect from all danger and harm, and restore you to us again in his own good time.

I forgot to tell you the result of our meeting. It closed on Sunday after you left, and on Monday seventeen were baptized and added to the school, among them our neighbor, Mr. Fanshaw. Your Ma, Archie and the children all send their love. Frank (brother) is on a visit to Moyock and will write you soon. Write him often.

Mrs. Shaw and family are all well. Tell Willie he must write me sometimes. Give him my respects and tell him not to forget his good resolutions and to never stop until he has obtained the pearl of great price. God bless and protect you my dear son is the constant prayer of our father J.B.M.

P.S. Ida sends you some money, $2.00.

"What is wrong with you, Jule?" I asked. "You look a little sad."
"Your dad said nothing about me in that letter."
"Ahh," said Willie, "poor lad. Fortunately, he does love me."
"He sure does, Willie," countered Jule. "He hopes you behave yourself and not drag his dear son down the path to hell."
"Shut up, Jule. You're so jealous," a smiling Willie quipped. "I say we have two dollars from your dear sister Ida. Let's go into Richmond and get some food and a little drink."
Jule looked at Willie with disbelief. "I can't believe, Willie, you are already trying to lead poor, innocent Patrick astray just after his pa asked you not to."
"Willie and I will go to town, and we will leave Pat behind so he can catch up on some Bible reading."
Both Willie and Jule said, "See you in the morning, Pat," and off they went. Not far behind them, they heard Pat trying to catch up. And when he did catch up, he said, "What Pa doesn't know can't hurt him, and what I know is the Lord is a forgiving Lord. The first two bucks are on me, with special thanks to Ida."
Every day, I thought about Pa and the farm. I worried that he needed me more than ever. I needed to go back home and help him. I was talking to Jule about my desire to go home and help my family. I was dismayed when he told me he was going to resign his cadetship and join the Confederate Army.
"What?" I said. "Where did this come from, as you have never mentioned you were thinking of joining up?"
"I know, Pat, but I feel that I must do more in this war. My family also believes that I can and should do more."
"But you just survived one battle. The odds are going against you surviving another battle, and you must realize the war is going badly for us. Please, Jule, don't do this," I begged him.

WHERE ARE MY FRIENDS AND FAMILY?

"Pat, I appreciate your concern, and I do agree the war is all but lost, but I must do what I can so I can hold my head up proudly."

"Good lord, Jule! What good are you if you hold your head up proudly and it gets shot off? You die for nothing. You have a bright future no matter who wins this war. Please don't do this."

"I'm sorry, Pat. I've made up my mind."

"What did you say, Jule?" Willie just came within earshot range of our conversation. "You made up your mind about what?"

"I've decided to resign my cadetship and join the army."

"When do we leave?" asked Willie, his eyes wide open with excitement.

"Willie!" I said as harshly as I could. "You know your ma is all alone on the farm and needs you home! The war is a losing effort now. What good are you to your ma if you get killed for a losing cause."

"Ah, shit, Pat. You could always take the fun out of everything. Jule, I wish I could go with you, but damn it, Pat is right. Ma needs me."

He left us in February and became a first lieutenant in the North Carolina troops corps General James G. Martin's brigade, where he served as a drill master.

The Yanks were closing in on Richmond, and word was they might attack soon. We were called out to man (March 1865) the trenches outside of Richmond today. Now I was concerned as I had seen what a real battle looked like, and if the Yanks attacked Richmond, it would be a bloodbath. We were so well fortified. The only problem was there was no food in Richmond. The Yanks had blockaded the ports and surrounded the city. They choked off all supply lines to the city. I believe when rats are considered the food of choice, it is to be considered a time to surrender.

It was late March 1865, and the rumor was that the city might be abandoned. I had seen people streaming out of the city for weeks now. Apparently, the Yankees were opening a way out of the city for civilians. I couldn't see a military solution for us. The troops were so hungry and exhausted that battle would be impossible. The cadets had not had a decent meal for months. All enthusiasm had perished in the corps, but we still sat in our trenches waiting for a Yankee attack. A Yankee attack that was not forthcoming as they knew they had us locked up.

I told Willie, "General Lee can't save us now."

Willie said, "We will be here until hell freezes over, and when they come, we will be ready."

I thought to myself, *Willie, you are a hell of a soldier, but you can barely stand up.* I looked at Willie. "Willie," I said, "this war is over. We can't fight without food, and that is the god-awful truth." Nothing much was said after that.

On April 2, 1865, the cadet corps was disbanded, and Richmond was evacuated by Confederate forces. The cadets were the last to leave Richmond. We were told to find our way home or elsewhere as best we could. Willie and I did not know which way to go. Yankees were everywhere around the city. Some other cadets were talking about heading out along the canal to Fluvanna County, Virginia, and dispersed there. Willie suggested we go with the group down the canal. I seconded it, and off we went, carrying everything we could gather up. A bunch of us cadets walked down to the Haxall Mills and found a barge. I noticed that Willie was walking funny. I asked him, "You are walking like you have a stick up your ass. What is wrong with you?"

"I've got my rifle tucked under my coat."

"Good lord, Willie, that rifle can get us all killed if the Yanks see it."

"I know, Pat, but I refuse to go without it, and nothing you say will change my mind."

"Damn it, Willie! You can be as muleheaded as any man I know."

"That being said, how can you hide a musket under your coat without being seen? I got a cavalry carbine rifle from a fella last week. It fits very well under my coat."

I'd never been so mad at Willie.

I said, "Just get your big dumb ass on the barge."

He looked at me like he might shoot me. I quickly added, "Please."

WHERE ARE MY FRIENDS AND FAMILY?

As we boarded the barge, a group of Confederate soldiers with torches were coming down to us. Were they going to burn the mills down? I could see some smoke up in the city from a distance, but I couldn't believe they would burn the city. As we paddled off down the Kanawha Canal, I yelled at the group, "Are you men going to burn the city?"

"Hell yes!" they yelled back. "The damn Yankees don't deserve to be in our beautiful capital."

My question was answered. They could burn down the city. I was glad to be on my way out of Richmond. Now if I could get to Fluvanna County without being captured, that was my next goal.

It was not a bad cruise along the canal. It was a narrow canal, and as we floated along, there were Yanks on the shoreline with guns, but they waved at us.

Willie said, "If I had my rifle, I could pick off so many Yanks."

Thank goodness we were told not to carry our weapons in the open. Apparently, word was given by the Yanks that all people who wanted to leave, including soldiers, could leave the city peacefully. You could not show any sign of weapons, or you would be shot.

I told Willie, "I know you would never try to reach for your rifle, as everybody in the boat would be killed or taken prisoner, right?"

"Yea, yea, I know. But to surrender like this is killing me."

"Well, you just keep your calm so you don't get the rest of us killed," I said with a half chuckle and half a fear that somewhere on this boat ride, he might take a shot at a Yank.

"Pat, I know, I know. I'm just saying," Willie said with a chuckle, keeping his rifle at his feet where he could get to it quickly if necessary.

Of course, anytime he saw a Yank in his mind, it was time to shoot and ask questions afterward. I stayed close to him until we made our stop in Fluvanna County, Virginia.

I was surprised as the trip down the Kanawha Canal was pretty uneventful. All of the folks on the barge embarked on the land. Everybody just stood around, wondering what to do next.

From within the group, a voice was heard. It said, "Who's going to Norfolk?"

I looked around, and there was Henry Whitehead. He was in the artillery with me. I said, "Henry, it's good to see you. I didn't see you board the barge. How's the shoulder healing up?"

"My shoulder is just as fine as the day I was born. But now I have a scar to show the ladies. I am a warrior."

Henry was a talker and very bright, but when his name was called for the artillery, I wasn't sure he could physically handle the battle. I was wrong, as even with his shoulder bleeding and his one arm useless, he continued to fight. I was glad to see him.

Out of the crowd came another familiar face. It was Cadet John Wise who proclaimed, "Henry wasn't the only one wounded at New Market. I got my warrior scar in battle too, and believe me, the ladies love it."

"That's great, John," said another friendly face. It was Cadet John S. Bagnall. He added, "I don't need no scar to attract the ladies. I have a personality to go along with my good looks."

That statement gave us all a good laugh as I personally had seen Cadet Bagnall embarrass himself trying to use that personality to impress many a fine young lady. I was glad to see my cadet friends. Now we as a group needed to figure out a way to get home. It seemed best to head toward Norfolk, and from there, our little group could disperse, and each headed out to their homes. I was feeling more confident with the five of us traveling together, but where do we go from here?

An older soldier suggested to our little group where we could go to find transportation by rail to head east. He suggested we head back down the James River to a town called Bellwood. "There, you catch the train to Petersburg. From Petersburg, you can catch a train to wherever. Say, boys, why didn't you just float down the James River toward Norfolk?"

"Well, shit," Willie said, shaking his head. "We were told to go up the Kanawha Canal to Columbia."

"Yea," chimed in Wise. "We assumed it was the safest route out of Richmond."

WHERE ARE MY FRIENDS AND FAMILY?

The old soldier laughed and said, "Boys, you just added two hundred miles to your trip home." He continued by saying, "Those Yankees gave us safe passage out of Richmond. Anyway, you wanted to go as long as you weren't armed."

"Damn it, Pat, what do you think we should do? Go with the large group or head out to Bellwood on our own? I think we should get back on this barge and head toward Bellwood."

We looked at each other with uncertainty, but what else could we do?

"Let's go for it!" Cadet Bagnall shouted.

So we jumped back on the barge and, with a shout, yelled, "All going down the river, hop on."

Off we went to Bellwood with no idea where to go from there. The float down the river was pleasant. We were stopped a couple of times by the Yanks, but we showed our cadet papers as students, and they allowed us to float on. Somehow, thank the lord, they never saw Willie's rifle tucked under the railing of the barge. I tried to talk him into throwing that gun into the river, but Willie was a big, stubborn man-child. I just kept reminding him to hide that gun at all times. He just kept saying, "Pat, we might need this gun, and I expect an apology from you when that need occurs."

We soon got to the town of Bellwood. We only found this little town by the lights of the houses along the river's shore. Cadets Bagnall, Cadet Shaw, Cadet Whitehead, Cadet Wise, and I hopped off the barge with a wave and a shout of good wishes to the rest of the boat. Off to town we went hoping to find some food. We had some money between us that totaled eight dollars. We headed to a little tavern that had a light on. As we entered, the man said, "We're closed." I explained to him we were cadets from VMI and that we were traveling home from Richmond. He wasn't impressed by who we were and repeated, "We're closed. Now git before I git my gun."

I pleaded with him. "But, sir, we have not had a good meal for weeks, and we have money."

"You have money, do ya?"

"Yes, sir, and we would love to spend it at your establishment."

"Take a seat. All we have left is a potpie filled with squirrel, rabbit, and some potatoes."

"That sounds great," I said. My mouth was already watering as I could taste that potpie.

The man left to prepare the meal as Willie said, "I wondered which side this guy is on."

"Does it matter?" I said.

"Damn right, it matters," Robert chimed in. "He could be poisoning our food."

"I think the worst he would do was spit on the food," I said with a smile.

"Since you are so sure, you take the first bite, and if you don't die, then Robert and I will eat."

"That sounds fair. Now hush. Here comes our poison delight."

In walked a handsome older lady who identified herself as the wife of the grumpy man. She looked at us hard for a few seconds, and all I wanted was for her to put that food down so I could dig in. Then she asked us if we were the cadets who fought at New Market.

Willie said, "Yes, ma'am, we sure are."

"Well, boys, this meal is on the house."

"What!" said her husband.

"Henry, these boys helped us win that battle at New Market."

"Well, I'll be a horse's ass," Henry said shamefully. "I thought you boys were Yankees."

"No, sir. Mister Henry, we are proud Confederates just come from Richmond."

"How's the war going? I heard we are holding on in Richmond."

"No, I'm sorry to tell you, folks, that Richmond has fallen to the Yanks, and we were the last corps to leave."

"Oh my good lord," Henry moaned. "That's the end then. I'm afraid the war is lost."

"Yes, Mister Henry, and we are trying to get home."

"Where would that be?" Henry asked.

"We all live in and around the Norfolk area, and would you, by the way, know if there are any railroads or means of transportation to go east near here?" Willie asked, hoping he knew something.

WHERE ARE MY FRIENDS AND FAMILY?

Mister Henry stroked his beard for a moment and said, "I know of a train depot in Chesterfield. It's about a ten-mile hike southwest from here. You boys can stay here for the night, and in the morning, after a good breakfast, you can set off to Chesterfield."

"You folks are too kind. I believe we will accept that invitation," Willie said with his mouth full of rabbit, squirrel, and potatoes.

The next morning, we got our things together, and after a big breakfast of eggs and potatoes, we set off to Chesterfield, but not before Henry's wife gave us a basket of sandwiches and water for the trip.

Wow, what luck it was to stumble into their tavern, I thought. The man upstairs was truly watching out for us.

We headed down the only road that went south. Our stomachs were full, and our hopes for getting home were high.

"Willie, I can see your rifle plain as day over your shoulder," I said in disbelief. "You need to get rid of that or hide it better."

"I will try to hide it better, but we need some protection out here in the country as there is danger everywhere, and mark my word, you will thank me."

"Just keep it hidden, Willie." I knew not to argue with him as he was as stubborn as any mean ass goat. But I was glad he was with us. After about five miles, we came to a sign that said, "Chesterfield five miles."

"What a relief," said John. "I thought we might be going the wrong way."

"John," I said, "I think the Lord is with us."

"I pray that you have been to church long enough to accumulate enough credits with the almighty to get us home," Willie said with a grin.

But I saw all the boys shake their heads in agreement with Willie. They used to make fun of my religious upbringing, but I truly believe that my friends believe I have some pull with the big guy upstairs. I pray that I do.

We set up camp outside of town. With a nice fire burning, keeping us nice and toasty, we sat down and ate most of the food given to us by Mister Henry and his wife back in Bellwood. Wise suggested we leave some of the food for breakfast, and we all agreed that was a good idea, so Wise placed the satchel up a tree not far from camp to keep the varmints from getting to it.

"What a nice evening for a campout," I said.

"Yea, it is, but where are we to go tomorrow?" Bagnall queried.

"We will catch the train and head toward home," Henry answered.

"Sure we will," Willie said sarcastically.

"We have eight dollars between us. I'm sure that will get us home. Listen, fellas, we will go as far to Norfolk as eight dollars will get us. Once we get there, we will figure out the rest," I said with confidence. Where that confidence came from, I had no idea. "Let's get some sleep. Tomorrow will be an interesting day."

I found a nice, soft place to lay my head down. The night was cool but comfortable. I wondered what my Mary was doing. I hoped she was thinking of me. What this war had taught me was life is short and sometimes shorter than you imagine.

"What was that?" I looked over at Bagnall.

"I don't know, but it sounds big, whatever it is."

"Henry, are you awake?"

"Sure am, Pat, and I heard that noise too. It sounds like it came from over where I hung the satchel."

Willie suggested, "It's probably a possum after our food. Wise, go scare that varmint off our food."

"Why me?"

"Because you know where you hung the satchel, dumbass."

"You don't mess with Willie when he starts cussing. Just go, Wise," I suggested strongly.

"Move it. Wise, as that bastard could be off with our food before you get there if you don't start moving your ass now!" Willie was irate.

Thirty seconds later, Wise came back white as a sheet.

"What's wrong? It looks like you've seen a ghost."

He stammered, "Bear, bear."

Henry, Bagnall, and I jumped up and went with Wise to the bear.

"Maybe we can scare it away from the only food we have. Good lord, that's a big son of a bitch," Henry remarked.

"No shit," I said. "Where is Willie?" About that time, that bear turned his attention to us. He decided he was not going to share his newfound food with us. We backed away slowly to show him we were leaving, but he kept walking toward us, baring his teeth.

"Boys, I just need to outrun one of you, so I'm running." Just before I was about to run for my life, the loudest blast came from the side. When the smoke cleared, there stood Willie with his smoking rifle with the biggest grin on his face. He looked at us for a while, just smiling. Then he looked at me directly and said, "Pat, you can thank me now."

"What took you so long to shoot?" I was nearly hysterical.

"Well, Pat, I only had one shot, so I had to wait for a good angle. I found a good level spot to take the shot, but the angle was not quite right. But I saw the bear walking toward you, and I was hoping you could bring him right into my sights for a kill shot. I sure didn't want to miss and have an angry, wounded bear."

"You sure as hell took your time!" I shouted at him.

"I got him, didn't I?" Willie said, a little disappointed in my attitude.

"Yes, you did, Willie. I am sorry. I have not been as scared since New Market."

"Seriously, guys, I needed to shoot that bear and kill it with one shot." Willie continued, "If the bear got one or two of you, then so be it."

We all jumped him and pinned him to the ground.

"I'm kidding, guys!" Willie shouted.

We lifted Willie up and had a group hug, and it was a true group hug as we had never felt closer than right at this moment. Willie's prophecy was fulfilled as I thanked him for bringing that rifle.

"But you still need to keep it hidden."

"Yes, sir, Cadet Pat."

Once we all got our hearts to stop pounding and could think straight, we looked at the bear to make sure he was dead. He was a big bear, at least five hundred pounds. I thought it was a good thing Willie had the gun, as he was as cool as a cucumber under pressure. I don't think anyone else could have taken that bear down with one shot.

"That being said, what do we do with it?"

"Cadet Whitehead, you are the smartest student here. What say you?"

"Why, Pat, I appreciate you saying that, but I don't have a clue."

"Maybe we could sell the bear to someone in the town," I said.

"Not a bad idea, Pat," said Willie. "But I think we should skin the beast for its fur and cut up the meat to sell in town. There might be enough money made for us to make it home."

"Great idea. Willie, but who knows how to skin a bear?" Bagnall asked.

"Never fear, my fellow cadets. Willie is here. I have watched him skin a bear," I said.

"Okay, I will do all the work, but if there is any money left over from our travels, I get it. Do we all agree with this?"

"Yes!" A group responded to Willie.

"Come on, Pat, you will help me."

"Aw gosh dern it, I hate that."

"Stop bitching, and let's get to work."

As I watched Willie skin the bear and then butcher it into fine streaks of meat, I had to ask, "Willie, why don't you become a butcher? You are great at it."

"I'm great at it because you know nothing about butchering, so shut up and pack up the best meat slaps in the satchel. Hang the meat high in a tree so we don't see another bear."

"I'll hang this hide to dry, and by first light, we can head to town."

"Good job, Pat. Let's get some sleep."

The next morning, we headed into town. First stop was at a mercantile shop.

"Sir," I said to the shop owner, "would you like to buy this bear hide?"

"Where did you get this? It looks fresh."

WHERE ARE MY FRIENDS AND FAMILY?

"Killed it last night," I proudly said.

"Well, it stinks, and it's not skinned very well. What do you want for it?"

"Thirty dollars," I said.

"I'll give you twenty dollars for it, and I don't dicker."

I gave Willie a look, and he nodded. "It's a deal. Sir, where would you go in this town to sell some fresh bear meat?"

"You say you killed last night?"

"Sure did."

"Then I might take the meat off your hands."

Willie was quick to assure the man he would have to pay for it.

"How much?" asked the shop owner.

Willie gave me a look with a shrunk of his shoulders like he had no idea what we should ask.

"What is your best offer?" I said.

"Ten dollars," he said.

I responded, "Pretty low."

"Take it or not, I don't care," he said with a huff.

"Deal," I said, feeling pretty proud of myself.

Bagnall exclaimed, "That was amazing. We now have thirty-eight dollars. Let's go to the train depot."

The depot was very busy for a small town. The tickets to reach Elizabeth City would cost each of us ten dollars. The train went to Petersburg, on to Norfolk, and finally to Elizabeth City.

"Boys, we don't have enough money," I said. "But where is Willie? Hey, Henry, have you seen Willie?"

"Yea, Pat, he went out back. He said he would be right back."

The time passed slowly as I kept an eye out for Yankee soldiers who strolled back and forth occasionally. They seemed to be a lighthearted bunch. The good thing is there was no concern on their faces for us, which I thought was odd. Finally, Willie came in, smiling like he just stole something.

"Where have you been, Willie?" I asked.

"Well, Pat, I'll tell you the god-awful truth. I felt bad about taking my rifle on the train, as I know you were very worried, so I went out back to ditch it. As I was sliding the rifle in a bush out back, I heard a voice say, 'What do you have there, boy?' My heart skipped a beat. I looked around, expecting to see a Yankee with a gun pointed at me. But it was an older gentleman just standing there. I said, 'What business is it to you?' 'Well,' he said, 'I was wondering what you were going to do with that rifle.' He seemed like a nice enough fella, so I told him the truth."

"You didn't?" I said.

"Yes, I did. I told him I was about to board the train and was told I could not carry a rifle on the train, so I was going to hide it until I came back in a few days."

"Brilliant lie, Willie."

"I know, Pat. Sometimes, I amaze myself."

"What happened next, Willie?"

"He offered me five bucks for the rifle. I said no, as this rifle is special to me. He asked if he could hold it. I said sure. The old gentleman looked it over real good and smiled. He offered fifteen dollars and pulled out the cash. I don't know because this gun took down a five-hundred-pound black bear. Oh, it did, as this seemed to impress the man. 'Okay, then I will offer you seventeen dollars for the rifle, and by the way, where is this bear you shot?' I said, 'It is at the mercantile shop in town.' The old man said, 'I would like to see that.' He asked, 'So what do you say, young fella?' I answered, 'I say, you got yourself a fine rifle,' and the money exchanged hands, and off he went with my rifle on his shoulder."

"You don't know it, but your rifle saved us again, Willie."

"You don't say, Pat."

"I do say this because we did not have enough money to take the train. The tickets were a sawbuck each. We only had thirty-eight dollars."

"So who is staying behind, or should we draw straws to see who stays?"

"Willie, you did realize with the seventeen dollars you just made, we all can get home. Your seventeen dollars gives us fifty-five dollars. We all can ride the train and have a half of sawbuck left for food."

"Hey now," Willie said, "that money is mine."

WHERE ARE MY FRIENDS AND FAMILY?

"I know that, Willie, but I also know that the gun you fought to take with you can bring all of us home."

"What do you say to me now, Cadet Patrick?"

"Thank you for bringing that rifle."

"I guess because I saved us twice now, I am a hero, and heroes should help those who need help. I will throw my money in the pot. That's the kind of man I am. But you know, this is just a loan, and when we all get back home, I expect to be repaid."

I thought to myself, *Willie, you are truly a rare breed.*

Willie and I joined the others, and I broke the news that we did not have enough money to get home. Everyone but Willie sank to a new low.

"What will we do?" John whispered.

I thought I better tell them what Willie did before the tears started to flow from my battle-hardened cadets.

"But there is good news." I put my arm around Willie's shoulder. "This man, among men, went out and sold his rifle, so we now have enough money to buy each of us a ticket home."

A cheer went up as everyone shook Willie's hand and patted him on his back. He was delighted to be the center of attention. Everyone went to buy their ticket home. Willie grabbed my shirt as I was going to the ticket booth.

"I want you to know I truly liked the story you told and all the thanks I got, but you will tell them when they get home that I expect to be paid back, right?"

"You know it, Willie. I swear on Grant's head."

I believed he was serious, but I would worry about that when we got home. All I could think about was my Mary back in Indian Ridge. I think I would ask her to marry me. Wow, words I never thought I would say, but war makes you think about how life is fleeting. The country was full of troubles, and our futures were unknown. I needed to get in line and get my ticket back home. On the train and going toward home.

After an uneventful train ride, we arrived in Norfolk, and it was time to say so long and good life to my fellow cadets, Whitehead, Wise, and Bagnall. I pulled over Willie and told him the guys would send the money for their tickets to him when they got home. Of course, I said nothing to them about owing Willie money. With handshakes and a lot of hugging, we left the boys with four dollars to split to help them get home. Willie and I didn't need the money as we could walk home from Elizabeth City. We were back on the train heading to Elizabeth City.

Once we arrived in Elizabeth City, it was only a twenty-mile hike to Indian Ridge or home. Hell, we used to march that far in a day, no problem.

It was the happiest moment of my life when the train chugged into the depot. Willie and I hopped off the train and just looked at each other for a moment. We started laughing and hugging, and people around us started to stare, so we composed ourselves. But we were full of joy and relieved to be here. Once the emotion simmered down, we realized that none of our loved ones knew we were this close to home. What a shock it would be to just walk into the house and say, "I'm back!" I couldn't wait.

Willie said, "Let's get going."

"Yeah," I said. "We have a good five hours before sunset, and we can camp in the swamp."

"That damn old smelly swamp. I can't wait," Willie said sarcastically.

We started off as soon as we got our few belongings off the train.

It felt great to be back in familiar territory, and it was a warm springlike day for a walk. We hoped to get a good ten miles down the road before we stopped for the night. After about two hours into our trek home, I heard a terrible noise coming from Willie.

"What the hell was that?" I said.

"Damn it, Pat. I'm hungry, and you know as well as I do when my stomach needs food, it will cry for it until it gets some. I can't believe you gave my money to the others. Now we have none for food."

"I'm sorry, Willie. I assumed we would just run home and eat then. Besides, Henry, John, and Bagnall had a longer trip to get home, and I knew they needed the last five bucks more than us. I could have been wrong," I said with the saddest face I could make, hoping I

WHERE ARE MY FRIENDS AND FAMILY?

could get some sympathy from Willie. I got no sympathy from Willie as for the next mile, he called me every name in the book. I think even his stomach was talking, and I could swear it was saying asshole. Thank the lord, an old Negro pulled up beside us in a wagon full of corn and apples. The old man asked if we needed a ride. Willie finally stopped chewing my ass and looked at the old Negro gentleman, then at the corn and apples in the back of his wagon.

He turned toward me and smiled as he said, "Pat, you must be tight with the Lord," and then to the kind old man, he said, "Yes, we would be very grateful for a ride."

"Where you headed, sir?" I asked. I could not believe it when he said Indian Ridge. "So are we," I startled the old man with my excitement.

"Well, then, hop on, son, and we'll be off. I need to get back by nightfall."

After riding a while, Willie turned to me and said, "Why don't you, Pat, say a little prayer for food? I could use something to eat."

"I don't think God works that way, but I will for you, Willie." I had no intention of bothering this nice old Negro by asking God if we could eat some of his crops.

He turned and looked at Willie and me, and with a concerned look, he said, "You boys hungry? You can dig into the corn and apples all you want."

"Sir," I said, "we could not eat your money crop. We have no money to pay you."

"No worries, boys, these crops were left over from the market, and I am bringing this to the hogs, so help yourselves. You look in need of food. The hogs won't know," he said with a laugh.

Willie looked over at me in relevance. I was afraid he might want me to ask God for gold or something, but he just started eating. Corn in one hand and an apple in the other. It was a most pleasant ride home as the Negro man introduced himself as Tom.

"What do you do, Tom?" I asked.

"I'm a free man," he said with a wide, toothless smile. "I have my own farm in Freedmen's Colony. I got me an acre of land, and I farm and fish."

I heard about that place, and I said, "How do you like it there?"

"I like it just fine, even though it's on an island. I own my own place. I'm bringing this food to feed my hogs. I even have a cow. Best milk in the colony, I swear."

"It sounds great, Tom. Willie and I will have to come and visit you. We'll bring some meat and fixings, and you supply the best milk in the colony. The least we could do since you are giving us a ride home with snacks to boot."

"You boys don't owe me nothing. Glad to do it. By the way, what are your names?"

"I'm Patrick Morgan, and this is William Shaw."

"Well, Colonel Shaw's boy?"

"Yes, sir," Willie said proudly.

"Mr. Joseph Morgan's boy?"

"Yes, sir."

"I'm pleased to meet you boys as your pas are good men." Tom looked over to Willie and very sincerely said, "I am so sorry to hear about your paw dying in the war. He was a famous man around these parts."

"Thank you, sir. He was my hero too."

"Well, boys, eat up and take a rest. We have a ways to go."

Willie and I got comfortable, and the next thing we knew, Tom was calling us to wake up.

"I'll drop you, boys, off here. We are in Indian Ridge, but I need to take the road going off here to get home to Roanoke Island before nightfall."

"Tom, I don't know how to thank you."

"You just bring a lot of food with you when you come to Freedmen's Colony. I have a big family."

We heard Tom laughing as he went down the road. The last words we could make out from Tom was "Bring my hogs some food since you damn near ate everything in the wagon."

"Thanks!" I yelled. He was gone, and Willie and I stood looking around. We are home. Willie shook his head, and I could swear he was crying, but I was not going to say anything. We went our separate ways as he went west, and I went east. I was a mile from home, and I ran the whole way to the house.

There in the darkness, the light from my home shone brightly. I couldn't believe I was here. I knocked on the door, and the door opened. There stood my pa. He looked at me without a word until I heard my ma yell, "'Who is it, Joseph?"

Finally, Pa snapped out of it and called, "It's our son." Then everyone ran to the door where Pa was still in shock and knocked me to the ground with hugs. Joseph (five years old), Ida (ten years old), and Ma. It felt wonderful. I asked where Francis was (eighteen years old). Pa finally spoke and very proudly said, "Francis is out with the doctor on an emergency call. He is studying medicine with Dr. Cowell." Then he picked me up and gave me the best hug I've ever had, except for Ma's hug, of course.

"We had no idea you were coming home, son," Ma tearfully said.

"The cadets disbanded on April 2 from Richmond. We were told to get home the best way we could, so Willie and a few others found our way back."

"Thank the Lord Almighty for returning our son," Pa continued. "You and I have a lot of work to do. With Francis out with the doctor, that makes you my new farmhand. Ma, fix this boy up some dinner. We will begin to rebuild tomorrow."

"I'm starving as corn and apples can only sustain a person for so long. Home sweet home."

My pa wasn't kidding about rebuilding, as without help, the crops would not be planted. I thought VMI was tough as I plowed five acres. I planted corn, beans, and soybeans. I was very pleased with my work. I barely had time to see my girl Mary. I usually saw her at suppertime since Pa had me laboring all day. One night at dinner, I told Mary I was worn out and Pa and I needed help on the farm.

She simply said, "Why don't you sharecrop out parts of your farm?"

"What do you mean by sharecrop? What is that?"

Mary continued, "Once the slaves were freed, a lot of the farmers couldn't find workers."

"Yea, so what?"

"Well, farmers started to rent small parts of their farmland to families who would work the land. The families paid the farmer a percentage of the crop sales."

That is very interesting, I thought. "I know where to find such families. Willie, you have all the fixings for a nice pork barbecue picnic?"

"I sure do, Pa. Let's get on down to Freedmen's Colony and get this hog cooked."

"I promised Tom a picnic, and we may convince some of the folks there to consider sharecropping."

Tom was waiting for us early so he could put the hog in the ground. I could see Willie and Tom had different ways to cook this hog, so I left them alone. I went to find Fred, my ole buddy. He was fishing.

"Hey, Fred, how are you doing?" I asked as he gave me a firm handshake and a big smile.

"It's good to see you, Pat. What brings you down to the island?"

"I know you heard about the picnic we are throwing for Tom this evening, Fred."

"I heard that. My family is coming."

"Good. We have plenty for everyone, but I have a question for you, Fred."

"Okay, what do you need? I know you think I am a fine fisherman, but I can't catch enough fish for the whole village."

"No, Fred, we brought plenty of food, but let me ask you a question."

"Sure, Pat, what's your question?"

"Are you happy here? Are you able to feed your family well?"

"Why do you ask, Pat?"

"I have a proposition for you, Fred."

"I'm listening, Pat."

"I want you to come back to my pa's farm and work the land."

"I already have land, and it is my land."

"I understand, Frank, but here is my spill. I will rent you two acres of land to till and maintain. For every crop you reap, you will pay me a percentage of your profit. This parcel of land you rent will be prime growing land, and you should be able to reap a much bigger crop. What do you think, Fred?"

"I would love to get off this island. I tell you what, Pat, let's talk over supper," Fred said with a smile.

"Mary Susan DeFord, will you marry me?" I hadn't thought about asking her that question, but the country was so dangerous, with the anger between families still festering and the gangs of men robbing and looting the weak who couldn't protect themselves. I loved Mary, and I wanted to protect her.

We married on July 19, 1865. What a great wedding! Family and friends came to wish us a happy union. My folks were concerned I was too young to marry, but they loved Mary, and we all lived on the farm. Mary had been a great help to Ma, and Pa was happy to have me home to tell me what to do. He loved to do that. But he was proud of me for my idea of bringing Frank back home on the farm. He was a good farmer and friend. His family came over once a week for dinner, and we had a nice visit. Fred had also gotten some of the other men from Freedmen's Colony to come over and work the fields during seeding and reaping time.

There was trouble in the Freedmen's Colony. The problem was by military order; they established colonies for the newly freed slaves on abandoned or confiscated lands. Under martial law, the White Southerners could not resist. This caused resentment among the white ex-landowners whose land was confiscated. People were also tired of the occupying military forces doing what they pleased. Several secret societies, such as the KKK and other groups, formed to fight these injustices done to the White Southerners. The times were getting worse, so I decided to read law with a lawyer in Elizabeth City. I passed the state board, but I never practiced. People in my community came to me to broker a dispute because they knew I was fair and knew the law. I was an instrument of the law but never took a fee. Maybe a pig or some vegetables or even some voluntary work around the farm, but never cash.

I decided to join the government instead of fighting it. I ran for the Currituck Board of Commissioners and was elected in 1872. The president, Andrew Jackson, ordered the return of all property under his Amnesty Proclamation, and the lands cultivated and occupied by contraband camps were returned to owners. The Freedmen were not given rights to their holdings in the colony; most left the island. Its soil had proved too poor to support many farmers. The colony was abandoned by 1870. I knew we needed to make laws to protect the newly freedmen and their families. Willie and I were talking about these newly freedmen who needed laws to protect them from the revenge of Southern White men. This anger was caused by good-natured Northerners who wanted the ex-slaves to move into society quickly by taking land from the White Southerners and giving it to the freed slaves. When President Jackson changed that, it threw a lot of freedmen's families in turmoil. I helped several Negroes families to sharecrop solutions. Fred was very helpful in showing them how well it can work. I told Willie that he should run for the North Carolina Senate. He could do more there, and everybody knew him and respected his family.

In 1874, he did, and he won two terms. During that time, he helped make thirty amendments to the State Constitution. Some of these were eliminating property qualifications for voting and holding political office, no more debt imprisonment, and public education for all Negro children. Willie was tired of politics, so he told me I should continue the efforts in the Senate. I was elected to the North Carolina State Senate in 1891 and continued trying to heal the country through legislation and laws. These changes in the laws were one of my most important contributions to the effort to heal my state. These changes had to be made so the next generation of Whites and Negroes could prayerfully live together. Unfortunately, there would be much pain and suffering, particularly by the Negro race. To educate an entire race of newly established Americans so they could survive independently would take generations to achieve. But I believe we have to start now if we wish to achieve this monumental task and save the country.

I got a letter from my old roommate, Cadet Brockenbrough. It was dated September 1866. The date today is 1880. I believed I missed graduation. How did that letter find me after so many years?

WHERE ARE MY FRIENDS AND FAMILY?

He said in the letter that VMI had opened back up and wanted to know if I was coming back. Apparently, only eighteen cadets returned. He said that the mail was not getting the letters delivered. I got my letter only fourteen years later. This got me thinking.

I made an application for the establishment of the first post office in Shawboro, North Carolina. I was made the first postmaster of this new office. Now I wanted to name the post office Shawsville after my good friend Willie Shaw's family. After all, Willie's father had been a doctor, lawyer, and congressman. But someone higher up than me named the post office Bailey. Where this name came from was a mystery, but I would get it changed. I was the postmaster general of Bailey Post Office until 1884. My good friend Henry Shaw took over the postmaster position in 1884, and by then, I had the post office renamed the Shawboro Post Office in his father's honor.

I sent out a letter to Robert Brockenbrough to explain to him I just got his letter a couple of months ago. I explained that this was the first letter sent out from the new Bailey Post Office in Shawboro, where I am postmaster general. "I hope this letter gets to you faster than your letter got to me." In my letter, I expressed to him my reasons for not continuing my education at VMI. These reasons were probably the same reasons for most of the cadets who did not return. Probably, most cadets did not get a letter. Those who did receive a letter were needed by their families to put their lives back together after the devastation of war. I did ask Robert to write back and tell me how the institute is doing. Also, I wondered if it would take his letter fourteen years to get back to me.

Believe it or not, a letter arrived from Robert four weeks after I sent my letter. Very fast! The letter was full of what had happened since the VMI cadets corps were disbanded in April of 1865. Robert reported in his letter what had happened in detail.

> The institute has rebuilt all the damaged buildings, and the institute has grown to over three hundred cadets. You won't believe this, but a senator in Congress by the name of Henry Dupont sponsored legislation to reimburse the insti-

tute in full for the cost of the rebuild. You see, Senator Dupont was in the Northern army at the Battle of New Market. He was impressed with the actions and bravery of the VMI cadets. He even sent two of his sons to the institute. I'm sure you have heard of Moses Ezekiel's monument to his comrades who fought in the battle entitled "Virginia Mourning Her Dead" (1912). It stands on the grounds of VMI. Every cadet's name is recorded on the monument. Moses is famous, believe it or not.

Two years after the battle, a detachment of cadets went to New Market and escorted the remains of the five cadets who died on the field of battle back to the institute and buried them under the monument beside Cadet Atwill. The six cadets who lay buried under the monument were Cadet Atwill, Cadet Crockett, Cadet Jefferson, Cadet Jones, Cadet McDowell, and Cadet Wheelwright. A plaque was placed behind the monument with the names of the other four cadets killed. They were Cadet Cabell, Cadet Hartsfield, Cadet Haynes, and Cadet Stanard.

Each year, on May 15, New Market Day is celebrated by honoring the ten fallen cadets. The entire corps is assembled on the field. The names of the fallen ten cadets are read off as a roll call. As each name is called, a cadet steps forward. I was honored to be chosen to represent Cadet Atwill. With a sharp salute, I reported, "Died on the field of honor, sir!" Flowers are placed on each grave. I tell you, Pat, not a dry eye in the stands. Twenty-one gun salute, followed by the playing of taps. It is an amazing display of respect for what we did. I want you to know that history will not forget us as long as VMI is here. You

WHERE ARE MY FRIENDS AND FAMILY?

must come up next May and see for yourself how magnificent this New Market day is. I hope you receive this letter sooner than the last one.

Pat, take care. We will always be brothers.

Your friend,
Robert

I couldn't believe that the people of Lexington and VMI honor us every year. I guess it was a big deal as I just thought we were like every other soldier who did what was asked of them. I remember times at school the frustration of not being able to fight. I think every soldier who did his job should be honored. War is truly a hellacious experience. There were 257 cadets involved in the battle. According to the newspapers that I have seen, ten cadets were killed, and fifty-one were wounded. Some of the wounded were severe and suffered from their wounds throughout their lives. I believe if every politician could experience battle, there would be a lot less war. Too deep for me.

For me, one of the worst moments came when my wife died. It was a cold night in November 1880. I sat with her the night she passed. Death is all around us every day as the disease takes many folks out here in the country. But I must go on as my pa did.

I remarried in September of 1881 to a wonderful, caring lady named Elizabeth Duke "Bettie" Ferebee. On September 11, 1883, my daughter Lettie passed from typhoid fever. She was the spitting image of my Mary. I would not have recovered from this if it wasn't for my loving and understanding wife. I have been very blessed to have a loving family to lean on in these tragic events. But it is a part of life, and we carry on. This is why the United States of America will survive and thrive. I believe that.

During my political career, I became acquainted with the Lifesaving Service. The Lifesaving Service was created along the beaches of the Outer Banks to save lives from ships that wrecked offshore. These stations extended from the Virginia line south to Hatteras Island. There were about twenty-nine stations. Each station was placed about two to three miles apart. They were manned by eight to fifteen men who lived there. They worked six days a week with one man off one day a week. If a man had a family, they lived in the nearest community close to the station and provided their own dwelling. Each station had a keeper who would pick his crew. These men saved many sailors from shipwrecks off the coast of North Carolina. A favorite motto the surfmen would often say was "You have to go out (to sea). You don't have to come back." Of course, this was not the official motto. I was offered a government job position to serve in the Lifesaving Service in 1897. It paid one thousand eight hundred sixty dollars per year. I was able to use my house as my office with a rent to the government of sixty dollars per year. The government did not want to pay rent for using my house as an office, but it happened. I was very happy to serve the government as long as they stayed far away from me. So this job sounded pretty good, and the extra money would offset any bad farming years. I took the job, and it made some memories for me. Let me explain what my job was.

I was named by the secretary of treasury with the Lifesaving Service superintendent's recommendation as a local district superintendent. This position was a civilian branch of the service. My job was to handle all the accounting (money) of my lifesaving stations in my district (seventh). I took care of payroll. All keepers reported to me of any surfmen not being at work or being sick. Also, any extra expenses that were needed for equipment, supplies, etc. I also had to visit each station three to five times per year to check on readiness, cleanliness, and recordkeeping. Some of these trips were pretty interesting, as I traveled from the Virginia border down to Hatteras, over sixty miles along the coast.

My first trip started in Elizabeth City as I boarded a boat to travel down to Kill Devil Hills. I got off behind the sand dune and walked over to the beach. I had a Negro man named Joseph who met me on the beach with a horse and buggy. The buggy had big wheels that rode on top of sand so as not to get stuck. We stopped at the Kill Devil Hills Station, up to Southern Shores Station, then south to check on Nags Head, Bodie Island, Oregon Inlet, Pea Island (Bad Mosquitoes), Chicamacomico, and so on. Tough trip, but the few

WHERE ARE MY FRIENDS AND FAMILY?

people living along the coast were very hospitable. I was invited into homes for food and water and to rest. I asked several people what they did to survive on this barren coastline. They just laughed and said, "Anything we can." But they got serious with me and showed me their garden out back, pigs and a cow roaming the beach.

Mr. Fulcher said he owned more animals, but they roamed freely and fed themselves. He leaned over to me close and said, "Our real treasures are what fall off ships when the ocean gets angry. Wooden boxes of wine or beer, cans of food, and sometimes, even animals swim ashore from shipwrecks. My pig swam in one morning. People have found plenty of old coins that wash up occasionally." He showed me a few coins he had found.

"That coin looks like a gold coin, maybe off a pirate ship that sank offshore."

"Maybe," he said, "but I have a few more things of value that I just as soon not show you."

"I understand," I said. "I hope the ocean continues to be good to you. See you next time I'm this way."

Mr. Fulcher told me I was always welcomed at his house. Like I said before, good people.

On my trip, I was amazed at the people I met. They were smart, hardworking, and honest to a fault. They relied on each other, so if one was in trouble, they all helped.

One interesting surf station (the Pea Island Lifesaving Station} was manned by Negroes. I asked to see the keeper, and a Negro came out of the station neatly dressed in his uniform and said, "Can I help you?"

I said, "Yes, I need to speak to the keeper as I am the superintendent for the Lifesaving Service."

"Nice to meet you," he said with a smile. "I am Richard Etheridge, the keeper here at Pea Island." I was surprised as I had seen only a couple Negroes at the other stations. Keeper Mr. Etheridge knew I was confused, and he began to tell me how he got into the service. He said, "I was a former slave who served in the Civil War. I returned to Roanoke Island and joined the Lifesaving Service. I was the first Negro to enter the service. I rose through the ranks and was promoted to keeper. Now the keeper hires his own men, so when the White men refused to work for me, I hired an all-Black crew. Last year, my crew and I rescued a three-mast schooner wrecked in a hurricane and saved every crew member on the ship."

I never heard about that rescue, I thought. Mr. Etheridge read my mind and said, "You will never hear about it because it was done by a Negro crew."

"That isn't fair."

"That doesn't matter, as my job is to save sailors, and that is what we do."

I have to say that his station was the best-kept station I have seen to date. On my first trip to the Lifesaving stations, I was struck by the job these surfmen do. They were on duty every day through snow, wind, and even hurricanes and what they call nor'easters. They walked the beaches looking for ships that had grounded or wrecked. Great people.

I will remember this day in July 1889. It was such a surprise. I was going through my mail, and there was an envelope with a letterhead stating it was from Virginia Military Institute. I thought, *Do I owe them money from my time there?* Surely, they were not asking me to come back to continue my education. I decided it was best to open it up and see what the school wanted with me as I gave it all I had in the two and half years I was there. Lo and behold, it was my honorary diploma from VMI. It was dated July 4, 1889. The letter stated, "Due to your heroic actions at the Battle of New Market and the burning of the school, the alumni association decided to award every cadet a diploma. We understand that many of the cadets could not return when called back nor even received a letter to come back to school. We are honored to have you recognized as a Virginia Military Institute alumni. May God bless you in all your endeavors, Virginia Military Institute Alumni Society."

Finally, I am now a college graduate.

In 1902, I was taking my usual trip down to the Currituck beaches to check the stations. I hopped on the ferry to Kill Devil Hills when I saw two young men sitting, drawing on a large piece of paper. I, trying to be friendly, asked what they were drawing to make

WHERE ARE MY FRIENDS AND FAMILY?

conversation. They looked perturbed as I disturbed them from their thoughts.

"What?" one of them said.

"I was curious as to what you are drawing," I said. "It looks like a large kite."

"Very good," the other man said. "Do you know much about kites?"

"No, not really. My name is Pat."

"Nice to meet you, Pat. My name is Wilbur, and this is my brother, Orville. We are heading to Kill Devil Hills."

"What's your business?" I asked.

"We are doing research on air flight."

I had to snicker, "You are trying to fly?"

"Yes, sir, and I think we are close to doing it."

"Where are you from?"

"Ohio."

"What do you do there?"

"Orville and I own a bicycle shop where we repair and build bicycles."

"From bicycles to flying machines. That's quite a jump in science, isn't it, boys?"

"I think he's making fun of us, Orville?" Wilber laughed as he said it.

"I like you, guys. Where are you staying?"

Orville said, "We have a camp set up near the sand dune in Kill Devil Hills."

"Well, you know, I come by that area a lot in my travels. I will stop in and see how this flying is going from time to time."

"Maybe," Wilbur said with a smile, "you have to look to the sky to see us."

Not in a million years, I thought. "I hope you don't kill yourselves." It was a very pleasant trip down the Albemarle Sound to Kill Devil Hills with these gentlemen as the more I talked with them, the more I believed if anybody could do it, maybe they could. Naw, if God wanted us to fly, he would have given us wings. I love dreamers.

The next year, I went down to the Kill Devil Hill Lifesaving station for my yearly inspection. The surfmen there told me they had been helping some brothers. They would help tote their kites up the sand dune. The surfmen were amazed to watch these brothers glide up in the air. I knew I had to stop in on my friends at their camp. Beside a shed was the biggest kite I ever saw. Orville was standing beside it.

"Hello, Orville. Do you remember me, Pat?"

Orville was startled. "Pat, you scared me as we don't get many visitors here."

"That is the biggest kite I've ever seen."

"If you hang around, you can watch Wilbur glide up in the air. We are about to take it up on the dune and do some tests."

"I wish success to y'all. Maybe I will stop back by on my return trip as I have to get going and make my inspections of the other stations. I will come back by tomorrow."

The next day, I returned to their camp. They were having dinner outside by a fire. It smelled great!

"What is that smell?" My mouth was watering.

Wilbur looked up and said, "It's an old recipe I got from an outer banker. It's a thick stew of flounder and shrimp cooked in a secret sauce."

"Let me have some of that," I said. The food was delicious, and after the meal, I asked how the kite flight went. Wilbur announced the flight was a monumental success.

He then looked me straight into my eyes and asked, "Do you want to see our flying machine?"

"Sure, Wilbur, show me your flying machine. Poor man, he's been staying out here too long in the wind and cold."

After all, it was December 16, 1903. He was thinking crazy thoughts now.

"Follow me."

Wilbur led me to a larger shed, and inside was a kite even bigger than the one the other morning. This kite was different. It had a motor and two huge propellers. Wilbur announced, "This is our flying machine."

WHERE ARE MY FRIENDS AND FAMILY?

"Unbelievable," I said, but I thought to myself, *I cannot for the life of me see this thing fly.* "It looks great, boys," I said, trying not to giggle.

"We plan to fly tomorrow if the wind is right."

"I sure wish I could be there and watch your beautiful air machine, but I've got to catch the ferry tonight. Good flying tomorrow, fellas." Those poor boys have big dreams. I hope they don't get hurt.

A few weeks later, I heard those boys actually got off the ground and flew. I didn't know where this flying idea would go as I didn't see much use in it. Can you imagine flying around in the sky? It's just plain crazy. They were nice boys, so I hoped they got some recognition for their efforts.

Once again, I received a letter from the Virginia Military Institute Alumni Society in 1904. This time, I could feel something inside the envelope. Inside was a bronze cross of valor. The letter said, "We have the honor of bestowing on you a bronze cross of valor medal, which was designed by your fellow classmate Moses Ezekiel." Son of a gun, what another surprise from the school alumni society. Our battle was gaining notoriety all of a sudden. I'd always been proud of the cadet corps for their bravery in the victory over the Yankees that day. We fought with and against a lot of brave men that day. I hope that battle will be remembered for the brave men who lost everything for a cause they believed in. I hope that people in the future remember how much suffering and destruction that belief on both sides caused. In hindsight, I hope people will learn from war how terrible the results are. The victors get their way, but is the destruction and loss of life worth it? A question that will be asked in future wars that I'm sure will come as man forgets history very easily. God bless this country as we try to become one America again.

Over the years traveling up and down the shore of Currituck County, I am proud and surprised by Negroes and White adjusting to each other as freemen. The Negroes live in the White communities and are given the freedom of working and raising families like everyone else. When a neighbor is in trouble, all the neighbors help, Negroes or White. I guess out here in the very rural and harsh environment of the Outer Banks, everybody needs help from time to time, and they rely on each other for that help. It's very pleasant to witness. Now all is not rosy, as there are still groups who fear the Negroes and want nothing to do with them. But I find very few Whites have that feeling who live out in the sparsely populated Outer Banks, where people help each other to survive.

I was happy to introduce my son, Charles Deford Morgan, to the Lifesaving Service on July 11, 1911, as my assistant. He was paid nine hundred dollars per year. He said he could use the extra money. I needed someone to make the long journey to inspect all the stations as I am sixty-seven years old. What a joy it is to have my son work with me.

I continued to work for the Lifesaving Service until it was changed to the United States Coast Guard in 1915. I retired to just being a farmer, hunter, and sometimes, lawyer to help settle local disputes. I never practiced law. I just helped people settle their problems.

In the forty-four-year history of the US Lifesaving Service, the surfmen responded to 178,000 lives in peril, and of those, they saved 177,000 lives. Quite a feat of courage. VMI made me the man that I am today by giving me an education and discipline. My love of people and respect for life came from my battle experience at New Market. The cost of war is devastating for life and property. It should be avoided and only used in self-defense. But I am afraid that wars will always be in our future as man is basically greedy. It is easier to take what's good than to work to achieve it. I hope that the Whites and Negroes can live together with respect for one another. I see it taking a generation or three.

*****

My great-grandfather died on August 27, 1919. He was buried in the Morgan graveyard beside his home in Shawboro, North Carolina. His house still stands in Shawboro today. God bless America, and may she always have men like my great-grandfather to maintain her.

WHERE ARE MY FRIENDS AND FAMILY?

My great-grandfather lived through the most devastating period of American history. How the United States of America was able to restore itself was because of ordinary good men like Patrick H. Morgan who believed in what America stood for and was willing to stand by his country even after a terrible defeat. Men like my grandfather did his part by helping rebuild his community. Men and women all over the country were heroes for restoring their local communities and helping each other to get back to living in peace. The war destroyed the country. The death toll and property damage were the most of any war America has ever had. The two sides fought against each other for five years. How did we survive as a country? Men and women went back to living free, and they rebuilt America. I don't believe any other country could have survived such devastation and hatred that war brings. I wanted to bring to the reader the feeling of how the Civil War touched practically every person in our young country. Our forefathers were people of faith, love of country, and, most importantly, independent people. These qualities were necessary for them not to give up on the idea of America. It was not an option. God bless them, for without them, we would not be the country we are today.

Postscript

My original purpose for writing this book was to tell the history of my great-grandfather. His name was Patrick H. Morgan. I wanted my children to know about him. His story is a reflection of the courage and resilience of the people in our country who rebuilt the United States after the most devastating period in our history. The Civil War. This is one man's story who made a difference not as a national hero but as a local hero to his community.

As I researched for the book, I was amazed at what he did. I decided to write this book not only for my kids and their kids to read but also maybe for all who have an interest in how this common man survived the war and came home to help his community repair the wounds from it.

Patrick Henry Morgan

Bibliography

Albemarle Genealogical Society.
Gerard, Philip. "Part 5 of The Civil War: Occupation of the East," Volume 4.
Gindlesperger. James. *Seed Corn of the Confederacy.*
National Park Service Brochure.
New Market Battlefield State Historical Park Visitor Guide.
The Heritage of Currituck County, North Carolina (1670–1985).
VMI Archives Catalog: Stories as told by the actual cadets from letters written home. Actual Letters written to PH Morgan from his father, Joseph Morgan.
Wright Brothers National Memorial, North Carolina.

On July 23,1903 at Henry M. Shaw camp no. 1304, North Carolina confederate Veterans met for a reunion near the Currituck County Courthouse and had dinner on the grounds.

About the Author

The author is a retired dentist who has been researching his family history from 1800 to 1899 for years. When he discovered his great-grandfather's life story, he thought, *What a story that would be,* so he wrote the story about his great-grandfather Patrick H. Morgan. The twist is the story is told as he is living it. The book is a fiction historical book.

Printed in the USA
CPSIA information can be obtained
at www.ICGtesting.com
LVHW091539221024
794497LV00002B/298